A Compendium of Unusual Tales

Ramsey Harrison

DEDICATION

So, you're bothering to read the dedication page? What's the point? You probably won't know the person or people that I'll dedicate this book to, right?

Wrong. I'm dedicating it to you. So what if we haven't even met? Maybe I know something you don't. Maybe I'll be the very next stranger you meet.

CONTENTS

ACKNOWLEDGMENTS

I'd like to thank the following people for their contributions, comments, feedback and support in the process of making this book a reality: Elizabeth Morris, Epru Husseyin, Amanda Callisaya, Rob Nutley, Brian Swift, Simon Himsworth and Janice Bowman.

1 JOURNEY TO RETURN

He got into the car and sat in the driver's seat. Pulling the hood down on his hoodie, he reached into the side pocket of his well-worn brown leather jacket. It was a warm afternoon for late October and wearing both the hoodie and jacket was making him hot, but he didn't want to walk around with the hood down, not now. He took the items out of his pocket and looked at them: a U.S. passport and an Alabama driver's license. The name on the license read, "Riley Hopwood". "I'm now Riley Hopwood," he said out loud. *What a fucking stupid name*, he thought to himself. He examined the license and passport closely and decided that they looked pretty good for being made at such short notice.

Riley put the license and passport back into his jacket pocket and took out his cellphone. It was switched off. He sat there staring at it, trying to decide if he should throw it out the car window. He had bought it from Paul some time ago, second-hand, as a backup phone. Paul was one of only two people he could call a friend, the other being Charles. All three had gone to the same high school together. Even though ten years had passed since high school graduation, they regularly kept in contact, mostly via the internet and mostly because of their shared enthusiasm for all things tech-related. Occasionally, all three of them would play online games together.

Riley had already carried out a factory reset on the cellphone and had a new, never-before-used SIM card, but he was worried that maybe, somehow, they could still trace it. Maybe they would speak to Paul and work out that he had the phone and trace it. *No*, he thought, *they're not that good. It would be a waste.* He switched on the phone and set up an account using 'riley.hopwood90' as his username, then downloaded a navigation app and set the destination as Niagara Falls. The app showed him a route and stated the estimated journey time as nine hours from his current location in Richmond, Virginia. His plan was to drive to Niagara Falls, dump the car, and cross the Rainbow Bridge into Canada on foot. He had some online contacts that claimed to be from Toronto, and he would try to get in touch with them once he got across the border. That was as far as his plan went. It was the best he could come up with.

He was nervous about the nine-hour drive. He was using a car registered in someone else's name with Virginia plates, and he had an Alabama driver's license. If stopped, he could claim he had borrowed the car from a friend, which was actually true. Charles had let him take the car, albeit indirectly, but then Charles might be charged with aiding and abetting because Riley's face had been all over the national news. He was a fugitive, and there was no way that Charles could claim he didn't know he was lending a car to a wanted man. After Riley had gone on the run, he had contacted his friend via a games chat room that he knew Charles frequented. Riley had accessed a restaurant's free public Wi-Fi by sitting outside of the building and using his laptop. He knew that the chat room was on a private server that didn't keep logs, so there would be no records kept of what they said. As soon as they both logged off, the chat history would be gone forever.

In the chat, Riley had explained his situation. Riley

wasn't sure if Charles had believed his version of events, but he had agreed to help. Charles would drive to visit his parents for the weekend, along with his girlfriend, in her car. He would leave his garage door down but unlocked, leave the car key on the workbench in the garage, and report his car stolen upon his return. When Riley asked what he would tell his girlfriend or parents about why he was visiting or using his girlfriend's car, Charles had told him not to worry and that he'd work it out. Riley considered the possibility that maybe it was a trap, maybe the police would be waiting for him at Charles's house, but when he got there, everything was exactly as Charles had said it would be. Riley's heart was racing when he removed the car from the garage—maybe a neighbor would see him and report a stranger—but the neighborhood was quiet and he didn't see anyone, so he thought that probably no-one had seen him.

Riley had collected the car on Friday night, both because he knew Charles would have left home by then, and also to minimize the chances of being seen. It was now Saturday afternoon, and he had just collected the fake license and passport from an online acquaintance he had done business with before. He knew that he had until late Sunday afternoon to ditch the car before it was reported stolen. It was a big risk collecting the IDs, but he felt he had no choice. The acquaintance, who had the online screen name MajesticHaxT3r, was surprisingly happy to help for the right amount of bitcoin. Riley had contacted him online via the Tor Network, which enables anonymous communication. This was how they always made contact. In the past they had exchanged computer hacking software, password lists, and all sorts of questionable computer data and code, until a relationship of sorts was built where they could trust each other enough to meet in person. Their few meetings were not, however, for the sake of friendship. They met to exchange bitcoin for fake IDs that Riley would sell on, or for acquiring hacking and other software that was too large to send efficiently over the Tor Network. It was ironic that the person he was now, Riley Hopwood, was a result of the same type of fake IDs he'd once used to buy and sell.

Why MajesticHaxT3r had no problems providing fake IDs to a wanted man who had been all over the news for the past week, Riley did not know. His character was such that Riley guessed he probably did not pay much, if any, attention to the mainstream news and probably rarely left his apartment. The photographs the national news programs had shown of Riley were pretty old, and MajesticHaxT3r didn't know Riley's real name, only his screen name. Even if he had seen something on the news, perhaps he simply hadn't put two and two together.

Riley put the key into the car's ignition and turned it. Other than Charles's car and the clothes he wore, the grand sum of Riley's worldly possessions now consisted of his cellphone, laptop, fake IDs, and 3,462 dollars in cash in a small tattered backpack, along with his intangible plan to cross into Canada.

Riley had been driving for some time and was making good progress on the route north, but he was now hungry and tired. Every time he saw a police car, his heart began to race. At one point in the journey, the traffic had narrowed down to one lane, and he could see flashing blue lights up ahead. He was sure it was the police conducting some sort of roadside check. He thought about ditching Charles's car by the roadside in order to avoid them, but knew he wouldn't get very far on foot. When he got closer to the flashing lights, he realized that it was just a traffic accident. The navigation app on his phone would have informed him of this, but he had exited it to conserve the phone's battery since he didn't have a charging cable. He would reactivate the app periodically to make sure he was still going in the right direction.

For the past week, Riley hadn't bathed and had been sleeping in abandoned buildings. He needed food, gas for the car, rest, and a shower. He looked down at his cellphone, sat on the passenger seat of his car, and double-tapped it to activate the screen. It was 6:26 p.m. The sun was setting as he approached the town of Bedford in Pennsylvania on the U.S. 30 highway. The road ahead was clear with no cars to be seen. After some minutes passed, he saw a sign for Bedford and decided to exit the highway. As he merged onto East Pitt Street, he sensed his eyelids getting heavy. He looked down at his phone and double-tapped on its screen again. The time was now 6:38 p.m.

As soon as the screen displayed the time, and before Riley had a chance to look up, he saw a huge, extremely bright white flash in his peripheral vision, accompanied by a loud whooshing sound. He glanced up as fast as his instincts allowed, in time to see something smash into the hood and windshield of Charles's car with a loud boom and then roll over the top of the vehicle. He applied the brakes as hard as he could, the car swerving from side to side as it came to a halt on the right edge of the road. "Holy shit!" he said out loud.

Riley got out of the car and looked back down the road. Something was laying on the ground about 40 feet away from him. His heart began to race again as he hurried over to it. As he approached, he saw that it appeared to be a person. Panic set into his body. He could hear the blood pumping in his ears. His first instinct was to turn around and get back into the car and drive off, but he quickly reconsidered. Leaving this person in the middle of the road could increase his chances of being caught, he thought, what with the damage evident to the front of Charles's car. He got closer to the figure laying on the ground. "Holy fucking shit!" he said again as he looked down on what appeared to be the figure of a young girl, maybe 14 to 17 years of age. She appeared to have some heavy costume makeup on her face and was dressed in what Riley guessed to be some sort of Halloween costume. It was late October, after all. He couldn't see any blood and didn't know if she was alive, but he had to be quick because he knew that if a car passed now and saw the scene, his arrest would surely follow.

Riley bent down, picked her up, and hurried back to the car. She was small and light, easy to carry. Her costume appeared to have elaborately made, butterfly-like wings folded down against her back. He raised one leg to help support her weight and used the fingertips of his right hand to open one of the car's back doors. Once she was lying down on the back seats, he closed the door and rushed to the front of the car to check the damage done to it. There was a large, circular, spiderweb-like smash pattern indented on the passenger side of the windshield, and a slight indentation on the hood just below it. The rest of the car looked fine.

Riley got back into the car and drove off. *What am I going to do now!* he thought. Those words kept repeating in his head.

Riley placed the girl down onto the motel bed and looked at her. He wasn't sure if he had gotten away with not being seen. He had parked the car as close to the room as possible, with its front facing some bushes to minimize the chances of someone seeing the damage. The motel attendant didn't seem too interested in him as he paid and presented his fake license, speaking in his best Alabama accent. He hadn't seen any surveillance cameras in the motel lobby and he didn't think anyone had spotted him carrying the girl from the car to the room, so perhaps he had gotten away with it so far.

She had what appeared to be intricate face paint applied to her whole face and neck, and fake-looking slightly pointy ears. The paint was a mottled beige, off-black and yellow pattern. Her hands had the same color pattern applied to them, and she had short hair, dyed bright purple. Her eyebrows were also colored purple. Her cheekbones were prominent and her fingers long and slender with black painted nails at the ends. The costume was very elaborate and looked well-made. It was black in color, other than the fluorescent blue highlights, and felt rubbery to the touch. He couldn't tell what she was meant to be dressed as. He thought she looked like a cross between a scuba diver, a motorbike rider, and a fairy. It was a very odd-looking costume, he thought. He couldn't see any obvious signs of injury on her, perhaps due to her makeup, but her costume didn't even appear to be damaged. He decided that that was probably a good sign.

"What the hell were you doing in the middle of the road?" Riley mumbled to himself, putting two fingers on her neck, checking for a pulse. He couldn't feel anything. He put his fingers under her nostrils. She was definitely breathing.

Suddenly she opened her eyes. Her eyeballs were black with bright red irises and large black pupils. Riley jumped back in shock. The girl sat up with extreme speed, extended her arm towards Riley with her hand up and palm facing him, and screeched something. As she did so, Riley felt himself fly backward as if he had been kicked in the chest. He hit the back wall of the room and slumped to the ground. He looked up to see the girl standing over him with her arm still extended. She started speaking to him in a language he didn't understand. Overwhelmed, Riley felt his vision blur and then everything faded to black.

Riley opened his eyes. He was still sitting in the same position slumped on the floor. He could hear a humming sound and could see the girl now sitting on the bed, apparently looking at his laptop. He tried to move but his legs and arms felt paralyzed. He let out a groan, and the girl turned to look at him with her piercing red eyes. She began to tap onto her right forearm with the tips of her left hand as if touch typing. The humming sound stopped and Riley felt that he could now move his limbs.

"Can you understand me?" the girl said still looking at Riley. The pattern of her speech sounded unusual. Riley was terrified. She wasn't in a Halloween costume at all. Whatever she was, she was real.

"Yes," he finally answered. The girl began to type onto her forearm again. Riley watched as her skin, eyes, and hair slowly changed color. Her hair turned a light brown, her eyes became human-like with green irises, and her skin turned a pale human tone. Her ears also appeared to lose a little of their pointiness. Riley sat still, staring in amazement.

"Is that better?" she asked. Riley didn't reply, so she continued. "Why did you bring me here? What is this place?" Her speech still had an unusual rhythm to it.

"I accidentally hit you with my car, and I brought you to this motel room to check if you were okay," Riley replied a little hesitantly.

"You struck me with your transportation vehicle and then brought me to an establishment that provides paid lodging on a short-term basis to check the status of my health?" she said. Riley was silent for a few seconds and then replied.

"Yes," he said.

The girl stood up from the bed and began to head towards the front door. As she did so, there came a loud crunching sound and the front door flew open, with bits of wood from the door flying into the room. Police in tactical gear, one with a battering ram, had just smashed it down and were storming inside.

Someone began to shout, "Police! Don't move! Stay where…" The girl pressed something on her forearm. A whooshing sound followed and then a buzzing filled the room. Riley looked on in amazement as the air in the room began shimmering, just like air shimmering above a hot road in the summertime. The fluorescent blue highlights on the suit the girl was wearing were no longer visible, and instead, thin pulses of green light ran up and down its surface. The police entering the room seemed to now be moving so slowly that it was like watching them in extreme slow motion. The girl turned to face Riley.

"Who are they, and what do they want?" she asked in

the same flat, unrhythmic tone.

"They're police, and they want me for something I didn't actually do! I don't know how they found me!" Riley said in a panicked and hurried voice. The girl turned back towards the door and casually began to walk out of the room, carefully stepping around each policeman as she did so.

"Wait!" Riley called. He stood up and followed her, bumping into a couple of the slow-moving policemen as he hurried. She was typing onto her forearm again as Riley caught up to her just outside of the motel room. Outside were at least half a dozen police cars and scores of police. Everything past a certain distance looked as if it was shimmering, and it was difficult to tell if the police were actually moving at all.

"Holy shit. This is insane." He turned to the girl who was still typing onto her forearm. "Wait. Wait... Where are you going?"

"I am leaving. I require energy," the girl said, looking up at him.

"I can help you," Riley said. "Take me with you. I can get you energy." He didn't know what she was talking about or even what he was saying, but he didn't want to be left behind when she went, in case the police went back to moving at normal speed. The girl looked at him for a couple of seconds before replying.

"This is wasting energy and time. Where is your transportation vehicle?"

"It's there, over there," Riley said pointing at it.

"Take me to Peach Bottom Atomic Power Station."

Riley took his cellphone out of his pants pocket and punched the destination into the navigation app. It was less than 3 hours' drive away. They got into Charles's car and Riley drove out of the motel parking lot, scraping along one of the police cars that was partially blocking their exit as he did so. After about 45 seconds of driving, the pulses of green light running up and down the girl's suit faded out, and the static blue highlights faded back in.

They sat in silence, driving, for about half an hour before Riley said something.

"Where are you from?"

"You are unlikely to comprehend where I am from. I do not have sufficient data to extrapolate a path between where I am from and where I am now, or how exactly I came to be here. My instrumentation is running low on energy and is unable to function at full capacity. I must acquire energy to process the data and attempt to return to the place that I am from. Do not speak to me further. I shall inform you in the unlikely event I need your assistance again. Just get me to Peach Bottom Atomic Power Station in the shortest amount of time possible with this mode of transportation," the girl replied.

"Okay…" Riley said. "Just one more question, what is your name?" The girl turned her head and looked at him with a blank expression. She then turned her head away again without answering.

"Right," Riley said, out loud but under his breath, "I'll call you Pixie. You kind of look like a pixie." Pixie did not respond or look at Riley.

Riley paced up and down in the control room of the power station. They had been in there for over an hour. They had been able to enter the facility with relative ease. Upon arrival, Pixie had simply walked in, her suit pulsing and streaking with green light, faster and brighter than it had before. Any attempts to stop her seemed futile. Guards or personnel that got too close were blown backward with the motion of her extending arm and open palm. Riley had instinctively followed her as she entered the building, walking only a few feet behind her. Anyone attempting to grab him was also somehow repelled. Locked doors posed no challenge and either bowed inwards before cracking open or shattered immediately as Pixie approached them. At one point, security began firing on them, to Riley's alarm, but the bullets seemed to stop in midair a dozen or so feet from them and fall to the ground. Now they were the only two present in the control room of the power station as alarms sounded. The lights in the room seemed to have become brighter after they had entered, and the dials on the control panels had all moved to their maximum positions. Finally, Riley turned to Pixie and spoke.

"What are you doing? You've been sitting there for over an hour," Riley said. The lights on Pixie's suit were now a purple color and were pulsing and streaking around her extremely fast as she sat on a chair, seemingly staring into space in silence. She turned her head to face Riley, and the lights on her suit faded out. The static highlights returned, but this time remained purple in color and not blue.

"There are too many variables," she said. "I do not have sufficient processing power to calculate a survivable return as quickly as I initially believed. But I have learned that I must construct additional equipment to be able to attempt a return. I am stuck here, for now."

"Right," Riley said, not knowing what else to say. He wandered to the end of the room and looked out of a window. It was dark outside but in the facility's lights, he could see a significant military presence. "Holy shit, half the U.S. military is out there. They'll try to stop you from leaving here," he said, turning to face Pixie. Pixie stood up and began to head towards the room's exit.

"That is unfortunate for the U.S. military," she replied, then stopped walking. "Are you coming?" she asked. Riley thought about it for a second.

"Yes. Yes, I am," he said.

2 CATHERINE'S CURSE

I think it all started when I was twelve. At first, I didn't understand what was happening, but as I grew older, I slowly realized. On the very first occasion I touch someone, skin on skin, something extremely strange happens. I get a vision of the last time that I'll see that person. I already know the last time I'll see my parents and my younger brother. Luckily, my parents will grow old. My brother isn't so lucky. When I touched his skin for the very first time, in the vision I got, he was still young, in his late teens. I don't know what will happen to my brother, but I assume he will pass away before my parents. I am seventeen now, and I have adjusted to this condition. Most people don't believe me when I say that I can see the last time I will see them as a vision in my head, and I have now stopped telling people about it. My parents believe me though. They support me and they will always be there for me.

When I was twelve, something tragic happened. I was still adjusting to my ability, trying to figure out what it meant, since it had only recently started as I went into puberty. I had made friends with a new girl, Julie, and I touched her hand. I saw a vision flash in my mind. In the vision, I saw Julie at school. She was talking to me and giggling. I then saw her get into her car, and that was it. I brushed it off thinking it was just my mind messing around with me again. The next few weeks went by, and Julie and I became close friends. My mom got to meet and know her mom when they would come to pick us up after school. Then, one day, after the bell rang for the end of school, Julie and I sat at the front of the school talking, waiting to be picked up. I remember we were talking and she was giggling about something I had said. Her mom picked her up from school, and she got into her mom's car to go home. I had a sudden sense of déjà vu. It was an exact replay of the vision I had seen a few weeks before. The next week, I didn't see her in school at all. One day, when I got home from school, I saw my mom and Julie's mom crying in the living room. They explained to me that Julie had passed away after getting an illness. I now know that it was meningitis. It had come on suddenly and had caused her brain to swell, killing her. I realized that the vision I had of Julie was the last time I had seen her alive. I remember thinking that night, *maybe I could have stopped this if only I had told someone about the vision.*

I don't have any friends because of this. My parents have tried signing me up for sports, but most sports involve physical contact with others. Most people who are friends share some sort of physical contact, whether it be a high five or a handshake. I try to avoid any contact like that. It makes me very depressed when I think that the first time I touch someone's skin, I will get visions of the last time I will see them.

I used to be a happy girl. I used to play and have fun. Ever since I turned twelve, I've been confused and lonely. Whenever I feel lonely, I listen to my music, and it helps me feel better. I also like to draw and write. I would like to become an artist someday.

"Catherine, come down for breakfast!" my mother calls out. I slump out of bed and walk downstairs. She prepares pancakes, and I drench my stack with syrup. I eat, and my brother slobbers while eating his pancakes. My brother reaches out for my arm. I pull away.

"No, Oliver, I've told you I don't like being touched," I say. He knows I don't, and he sometimes does it to annoy me.

"Oliver, leave your sister alone," my mother says.

"It's not fair. You're no fun, Catherine," Oliver says, crossing his arms. I finish my pancakes, go back upstairs, and get ready for school.

After I get ready, I grab my backpack and walk towards the door. I open up the door when my mom calls for me.

"Catherine?"

"Yes?" I reply.

"Can I give you a kiss today?" she asks.

"No," I say and slam the door. I walk and take a right away from the houses, into the forest, and away from other people. The forest welcomes me with a big smile. The trees shiver to the song of the wind. I hear nothing but the sound of my feet trudging through mud. The leaves gently float to the ground. Snot drips out of my nose, and I wipe it onto my sleeve. The cold wind freezes my ears, and my hands go numb. I pull black gloves out of my pocket and put them on. The gloves will block me from seeing visions when I touch someone but, occasionally, even when I wear gloves, I still get a vision when I touch someone for the first time. Why? I don't know.

I get to Liberty High School, and I sit in my math class. School goes by slower than a snail. After school, I decide to go to the store. I get there and walk around. I notice that a lot of people are in the back crowding around something. I walk over there and finally get to the front of the crowd. There are boxes stacked up of brand-new wireless headphones that have just recently come out onto the market. They have already been discounted which is a little odd, but they are selling fast, so I purchase a pair on impulse and open them up in the store. Taking off my gloves, I put the headphones around my head. I sync them with my cellphone and turn on my music. I'm walking to the front of the store when suddenly, someone's cart bumps into me. My hand falls onto the other person's hand, and I freeze there for a moment. Nothing happens. I don't see a vision. *Wait, what just happened? Why isn't there a vision?*

"May I help you?" the boy with the cart says, and pulls his arm away. He has dark brown, almost black hair and chocolate brown eyes, and he looks roughly my age. I turn my music down. I suddenly feel panicked and dazed as if my head is spinning. Why wasn't there a vision?

"Uh, oh my gosh, I'm so sorry. I didn't mean to bump into you. Do you have a problem?" I stutter. He laughs at me.

"Do you have a problem?" he says back with a slight smile.

"N-No, I just didn't see anything," I say. He stares into my eyes. I can feel my heart racing in my chest. I just touched someone and nothing happened!

"Your eyes look pretty fine to me," he says, chuckling. He smiles at me, and I smile back nervously.

"I'm sorry again for bumping into you."

"It's okay. You seem pretty nice."

"Thank you," I say, and blush. He scribbles something on a piece of paper, rips part of it off, then hands it to me. *Who carries a pen and paper in their pocket like that?* I think to myself. Then I guess that he probably used them to make a shopping list before coming to the store, and still has them.

"Message me if you want. Maybe we can go out for pizza or something," he says. I look down at the piece of paper. It has a number written on it which I assume is his cellphone number.

"Sure, I'd love that," I say. He holds out his hand for me to shake. I pause for a few seconds, looking at his waiting hand and then at his face, before I nervously grab it. No vision!

"My name is John; what's yours?" he asks.

"Catherine," I say.

"Well, nice to meet you, Catherine," he says, then walks away to continue shopping.

I giggle to myself and leave the store. I walk home in the dark and can't stop myself from smiling the whole way.

I get home and the smell of chicken wafts into my nose.

"Dinner is ready!" my mom yells up to my brother. I put my backpack down and sit at the dinner table. There are potatoes and beans and mac and cheese placed out on the table. Oliver comes downstairs, and Dad comes in from the living room. My dad has left the television on. A news channel is playing. I'm chowing down on some potatoes when the television catches my attention.

"Coming up next tonight, the story on the recall of the newly released iBuddy wireless headphones. Customers are saying that the headphones have been giving them severe headaches after a short period of use. iTech, the company that manufactures the headphones, states that whoever has bought these headphones should return them immediately," the news anchor says. "ZKB News has learned however that some unscrupulous retailers, fully aware of the problem with these headphones, have still been selling them at a discounted price to get rid of their stock as soon as possible. Now, iTech has finally caved in and ordered a costly recall. We spoke with one mother who says her son has been having headaches after using the headphones. They have been so severe that…"

I lose concentration on what the news anchor is saying and drift into my own thoughts. I unknowingly drop the spoon I am holding. It lands on my plate. *That's what went wrong at the store today*, I realize, *the headphones stopped me from seeing a vision.*

After dinner, I grab my headphones and run outside. I walk a short distance away from my house and wait for a stranger to walk past me. When one finally does, I approach him from behind and touch his hand. I instantly see a vision of this person saying something to me and then walking away, occasionally looking back at me with a bemused expression. Immediately after the vision, the stranger turns toward me and says,

"Hey, what are you doing?" He walks away from me, looking back at me occasionally with a bemused look on his face. I then put the iBuddy headphones on my head and switch them on without playing any music. I wait for a minute or two in the street, find a different person, and touch their hand. This time nothing happens. No vision.

"What the hell are you doing, young lady?" the man says, pulling his arm away.

"I'm sorry. I thought you were someone else," I say and hurry back home.

I run upstairs to my room and pull my cellphone out. I message John and wait for him to reply.

"Hey, it's Catherine," I type.

"Hey, Catherine," he types back.

"How are you?"

"I'm good, how are you?"

"Good."

"Would you like to go out to Tony's Pizza Parlor at the mall after school tomorrow?"

"Yes."

"Alright see you then." He sends a smiley face at the end of the text.

I giggle to myself and bury my face into my pillow. I finish my homework, then get some rest.

When I wake up, I go to the garage and get black electrical tape from my dad's toolbox. I cover the iBuddy logos on my headphones with the tape. I know that the headphones have been on the news, and I don't want anyone to approach me and talk to me about them. I then jump into the shower, get dressed in a pink skirt and a matching top. I walk downstairs, and my mom hands me a bowl.

"You seem really happy today," she says.

"Can I go out today with a friend?" I ask.

"Oh, sure, that's exciting!" she says, a little surprise mixed with happiness showing in her voice. "Please be back by eleven. I don't want you out too late," she adds.

"Okay, mom," I say.

I grab my backpack, go up to her and kiss her cheek, my dislike of physical contact diminished. I walk out the door and head to school. I get there and can't stop smiling. I can't wait to go out tonight. I've never been this happy about anything.

After school, I walk to Tony's Pizza Parlor. I put my gloves on since it's cold out. I arrive a little early and have been standing outside the restaurant for about twenty minutes when, finally, John arrives.

"Catherine," he says and smiles.

"John," I reply.

He opens the restaurant door for me, and I walk inside. We grab a booth and sit down. The waitress brings us the menu.

"What kind of pizza would you like?" he asks me.

"I like mushroom and sausage," I say.

"Alright, mushroom and sausage it is."

He orders the pizza and a glass of water for each of us. The water arrives first, and I take a sip from my glass.

"So, have you bumped into anyone recently?" he laughs.

"No," I say and laugh with him. Soon the pizza comes out and I take two slices onto my plate. I take a bite and a mushroom falls onto my lap. I pick it up and pop it in my mouth.

"You go to Liberty High, right?" he asks.

"Yes, how did you know?" I reply.

"Just a guess. I'm over at Riverrun High, and since you

don't go there, I figured you might be at Liberty," he says.

"Yeah," I say and nod.

"So, tell me. What do you like to do?" he asks.

"I like to listen to music and paint," I say.

"That's cool," he says. "Maybe I could see your paintings sometime?"

"Yeah, sure, I have a few photos of my artwork on my phone," I say and pull out my cellphone.

I open up the gallery app and scroll through the photos until I find the ones of my paintings. I show him my painting of a girl sitting on a windowsill in the dark and he grins.

"These are really good. I'm not very good at painting or drawing," he says.

"Yeah, I paint my feelings. Sometimes a feeling is so complicated that I can express them better through my art than through using words."

"I understand," he says. "Art has its own sort of expressive power."

"I also like to write and listen to music."

"What kind of music?" he asks.

"I love listening to Storm."

"Oh, no way! I love Storm. They're my favorite group," he says.

I keep the headphones switched on and around my neck, but without any music playing.

After our dinner, he walks with me to my house. We talk about school, and he tells me about his baseball team. We get to my door and I turn to face him. I adjust my headphones and he chuckles.

"Today was really fun. I'd love to see you again Catherine," he says.

I smile. "Maybe we can see each other soon?" I ask.

"Yes, that would be awesome," he says.

He reaches for my face and gently touches my cheek. I blush, and he gives me a warm smile. He takes his hand off my cheek and holds my hand. No vision. I let go of his hand, take off my headphones, and switch them off before putting them into my bag. I take a deep breath and move closer to John. I stand on my toes and, knowing what will happen next, kiss John gently on his lips.

3 JOANNE

Joanne was a loud girl. She had been the loudest in her group of high school friends and was always getting into trouble. Being loud and pretty inevitably attracted the boys, but they always seemed to be the wrong type of boys, always loud themselves, who didn't take their schoolwork or future prospects seriously.

Joanne's first boyfriend was a boy named Peter Feldman. Peter was a loud boy that liked to show off and generally act foolishly to attract attention, and it seemed to work. He had attracted the attention of Joanne when they were both fifteen and still in high school. He had flicked food onto Alex Weaver from across the school cafeteria and everyone had laughed. Poor Alex was a quiet, shy boy and didn't know who had thrown the food at him from behind his back. Everyone had giggled and made fun of him for the rest of the day as he passed them in the hallways or sat with them in his classes, his sweater still showing the off-yellow food stains from the mac and cheese that had landed on it.

Why this sort of behavior was attractive to Joanne, she did not know, but the fact was it had been. The very next day, when Peter had asked her if she wanted to go to the cinema with him, she found herself saying yes. She already knew that they lived in the same neighborhood of East Redstone. She had occasionally seen him in the area on his bicycle with his group of friends, not that Joanne and Peter were themselves friends or anything of the sort.

The first few weeks of their relationship had been fine. They had played games on Peter's games console in his bedroom on the weekends and after school. Joanne was enjoying having a boyfriend and felt like she was growing up, but after a few weeks Peter began to change. He started being rude towards Joanne and began asking her to do things she wasn't comfortable with. When they kissed, he would try and put his hand down her pants and into her underwear. Joanne had told him on multiple occasions that she just was not ready for that, but Peter simply became more and more of a bully.

Finally, Joanne agreed to allow Peter to photograph her breasts and genitals on his cellphone. Peter had explained to Joanne that if she wouldn't let Peter touch her down there, like most other girlfriends would, the least she could do was let him take pictures of her so that he could use them to 'relieve' himself when he was alone. Joanne, in her foolishness, eager to please Peter, thought that this was a fair compromise, but the very next day at school, Peter's friends began making odd sounds and shouting, what Joanne perceived to be, random words in her direction whenever they were close by. Finally, as everyone was leaving at the end of school, one of Peter's friends, Jordan Merriman, shouted out at her from across the school courtyard,

"Hey Joanne, I love your lips, even though one of them is much bigger than the other," and he pulled his bottom lip down with his forefinger and thumb. Peter along with all of his friends began to laugh. Joanne ran from the school courtyard crying, realizing what Peter had done. He had shown all of his friends the photos he had taken of her.

The teasing went on for weeks before Joanne finally

broke down one morning and refused to go to school. She refused to tell her mother what was causing her the anguish, so her mother signed her up for therapy sessions.

Dr. Ramsden, her therapist, was a good man, Joanne thought. He was kind and caring and mature. He listened when she spoke and he genuinely cared. Joanne saw him twice a week after school. Over time he slowly brought Joanne's confidence back out. He explained to her about the broader aspects of the world, the realities of teenage drama and the phases of life that almost all people went through. Finally, he had told Joanne about 'the shadow'.

Dr. Ramsden explained to Joanne that the shadow was a psychological concept developed by Carl Jung, a Swiss psychiatrist and psychoanalyst.

"The basic concept is as follows," Dr. Ramsden had said. "Imagine that you are told that aggression or anger are bad emotions and that you should try to suppress them whenever they arise. What you will be doing is trying to suppress emotions that are innate and natural. These are emotions that have been built into all of us by evolution over countless years. These are emotions that are found, not only in humans, but throughout the animal kingdom. Eventually, nature will win out and these emotions, that you have been fighting so hard to suppress, will burst through to the surface, perhaps in unpredictable and unpleasant ways. Plus, there are times when it is perfectly reasonable to be aggressive or angry. It is far better to integrate these emotions, integrate your shadow, your dark urges. Don't ever tame your demons, but always keep them on a leash."

Joanne felt a lot better after her therapy sessions with Dr. Ramsden. She did her best to learn from his advice and his therapeutic methods seemed to be helping. It was around this time that she developed a crush on Dr. Ramsden. In fact, she had gone off boys altogether and found herself being attracted to older men in general. She would never act on her crush. She respected Dr. Ramsden too much to do anything foolish or embarrassing, and the last thing she wanted was to potentially get someone that had helped her so much into trouble.

Some weeks after Peter had shown the photos of Joanne to his friends, and after Joanne's therapy sessions with Dr. Ramsden had been reduced to once a week, things at school had calmed down a little. Joanne still got comments occasionally but with Dr. Ramsden's help, she seemed to be coping well.

Things changed even more drastically a few weeks after this, when Peter was found dead at the bottom of a tree in the woods behind his house. By all accounts, he had been climbing it when he fell and broke his neck. He had sent a text message to his friends to come and meet him there. When the first of them had arrived, Jordan Merriman, he had found Peter there, dead on the ground below the tree he used to regularly climb with his friends, next to his bicycle.

Everyone at school forgot about the photos of Joanne after this. Everyone at school only spoke about the tragedy that had befallen poor Peter. Joanne did her best to feel sorry for his family and friends, she said the right things to the right people if they ever asked her about her dead ex-boyfriend, but deep down she was happy he was dead. She was happy no-one was talking about the photos anymore and she embraced the feeling she got when she thought about his neck snapping as his head hit the ground. She would soon be the loud happy Joanne once again, she had thought to herself at the time.

Joanne received a phone call in the morning to inform her not to turn up for work. During the weekend there had been an explosion at the paint factory. Apparently, no-one had been hurt. She was not told any more than that, but she really didn't care. As far as she was concerned, she was 19 years old, still lived at home with her mother, didn't have to pay any bills, and now didn't have to go into work. She reasoned her job would still be waiting for her when the factory reopened.

On top of now being unemployed, she was having relationship problems with her current boyfriend, Steven. They had been together for about six months and had met at a gym, local to where they both lived. Their relationship seemed to deteriorate after Joanne had started working at the paint factory, a couple of months ago. She was excited about leaving high school and getting her first full-time job. She worked there as a receptionist. It wasn't unusual for the factory to frequently be visited by potential customers looking to make large orders. There was a paint store at the same location as the factory, owned by the same corporation, but some customers planning on making large orders wanted to see the workings of the factory, and she would be the one to greet them as well as answer any incoming calls along with another receptionist.

Her boyfriend, Steven, was a slow-witted jock-type who was six years older than her. When Joanne thought about it, the only reason she could remember as to why she had got together with him in the first place was because of his age.

She found herself being more and more irritated by him. Joanne had been thinking about the situation, going over it in her head. Recently, he had threatened to email her parents pornographic photos he had taken on his cellphone of them together. These were taken early on in their relationship when things were exciting, fun and new. It seemed as though history was repeating itself and that she was making the same mistakes with Steven as she had with Peter.

She had tried to break up with him on a couple of occasions, but he would either act very sorry and loving towards her, or if that didn't work, resort to threats.

Joanne had decided she had had enough. She thought back to her therapy sessions with Dr. Ramsden. She had a right to be angry, she had a right to be aggressive, she had a right to get him out of her life. It was time for her to unleash her demons. She had been thinking of ways to get rid of him. But how could she do this and be sure he wouldn't follow through on his threat to send their homemade porn photos to her family or post them onto the internet? Now that she was temporarily unemployed and had free time, this was the perfect opportunity for her to come up with a plan to dump him and execute it.

Robert's cellphone rang and he looked at the number displayed on its screen. He didn't recognize it. *I should ignore it*, he thought, but answered it anyway.

"Hello?" Robert said, but the line was quiet with only some slight rustling sounds to be heard. "Who is this? Hello?" Still only the rustling noises. "Look, whoever you are, if you call me one more time, I'll call the pol…" but it was too late, the caller had hung up. Robert had been receiving these calls for some time now and he was getting more and more annoyed with each one. Whoever was calling him used a different number each time. If Robert tried to call the number back, as he had done on a couple of occasions, an automated voice would inform him that the number he had dialed was invalid.

Recently Robert's car had been stolen and now, having heard that morning what had happened at the factory and knowing that there would be no work until it reopened, he was feeling very low.

Robert was a pleasant man. He was a foreman at the paint factory and got on well with most people so he could not think who might be making the calls. At 37 he looked good for his age, but he was not getting any younger and with his financial responsibilities, he couldn't afford to wait for the factory to reopen. His insurance wouldn't cover his situation, so he would have to find some other employment until the factory reopened. Robert huffed to himself and decided to go buy a sports car magazine from the local 7-Eleven.

Joanne placed an assortment of items onto the payment counter of the couples boutique.

"Will that be everything, Miss?" the man behind the counter said.

"Could I also have that long brown wig, the red wig, the French maid's outfit, and the nurse's uniform?" Joanne replied, pointing to the items hung up on display behind the counter clerk, one by one. The man smiled.

"I see," he said and stared at her for a while with a grin on his face.

"A friend and I are going to a fancy-dress party tonight," Joanne added.

"Oh, I see," the clerk said and his grin got bigger. He was in his late 30's and Joanne noticed that his hair looked greasy. "Did you know that those two outfits are our most purchased by women? I wonder why?"

"Look, could you hurry up please. I'm in kind of a hurry." Joanne didn't like the clerk's creepy attitude. The man put the items in a bag and placed the bag onto the counter.

"That will be $179.72 with tax. You know it would be cheaper if you bought outfits from a fancy-dress store. Unless you plan on using them regularly, if you know what I mean?" he added in a slimy voice. Joanne did not reply. She simply placed $180 on the counter and took the bag, turned around and began to walk out of the store without waiting for her change.

"What about your receipt?" the clerk called after her. She ignored him and left.

Steven stumbled, barefoot and half awake, from his front door to his mailbox. He retrieved his mail and went through it, finding mostly junk mail, until he came upon an envelope with no markings on it. It must have been placed into his mailbox by hand. He opened it. There was a card inside that had on it an illustration of two sad puppies looking at each other. On the back, it read,

We need to sort things out. Meet me outside of the Best Western Hotel on Mathis Ave at 8:00 p.m. It's a surprise. I will explain everything. Bring this card to claim your surprise and don't tell anyone about this.

At last, Steven thought to himself. He had been trying to get back on to good terms with Joanne for over a week and it seemed as though something he had done had finally worked. All of a sudden, he felt a nervous anticipation and could not wait for it to become eight o'clock. He looked at his watch. It was only 9:03 a.m. He would go shopping and buy new clothes for tonight's big date, he thought to himself, then stuffed the card back into its envelope and the envelope into his back pocket. He ran back into the house to get fully dressed and to get his wallet. At no point did he notice that the card had not been signed or that the handwriting on it was not Joanne's.

As Robert left the 7-Eleven, he had the oddest feeling that someone was watching him. He turned and looked around. There were a few people standing outside of the 7-Eleven and a few walking behind him in the same direction he was. He rolled up the sports car magazine he had just purchased and placed it into the inside pocket of his jacket. As he continued to walk, the feeling of being watched came again. Robert deliberately slowed his pace. As he felt someone approach him from behind, he turned around and grabbed the person behind him, catching him by the scruff of the neck.

"If you don't tell me why you are following me..." Robert began to say, then stopped. An elderly man was looking back at him, terrified. The old man looked as if he was about to have a heart attack. Robert let go. "I'm sorry, I thought..." he tried to explain, but it was pointless. The man turned and ran off as fast as he was able in the opposite direction, occasionally looking back to make sure he wasn't being pursued. The people in the street who had seen the incident briskly walked away from Robert's vicinity, fearing that this unhinged individual might attack them next. Embarrassed by his actions, Robert too hurried away from the scene.

Upon returning home, Robert had no sooner entered his house than his cellphone rang. He retrieved the phone from his pocket and looked at it. Again, a number he didn't know was calling. "Hello!" Robert answered it angrily. This time someone actually replied.

"Do you know the things we could do together?" a voice came back. Robert could not tell whether it was male or female. It had been disguised electronically. "We could have all sorts of fun and…"

"Listen," Robert interrupted, "I don't know what the idea is, but this isn't funny and if you—" The caller hung up. "Grrr!" Robert growled in annoyance. He shoved his cellphone back into his pocket and went to try and calm down by reading the magazine he had bought.

Later that evening Steven stepped out of the shower and began singing to himself, out of tune. He was horribly mashing different songs together.

"Baby you're all that I want… I gotta feeling… Nobody does it better… Simply irresistible…" He couldn't stop smiling as he dressed in his newly purchased clothes.

The time was now 7:00 p.m. and Steven sat waiting anxiously for an Uber to arrive. Someone had slashed all of his car's tires the previous week. It has sent Steven into a rage when he had discovered the four deflated tires. He didn't have the money to repair them until the end of the month when he got paid, so he had been borrowing his mother's car to get around in, and for commuting to work. However, his mother's car was pretty old and a little beat up, so he didn't want to use it to drive to the hotel. This was his big chance to win Joanne back. No, he had decided, he would rather use an Uber to get to the hotel.

Steven slapped aftershave onto his face for the third time and kept looking at himself in the mirror every two minutes. The Uber arrived and stopped outside of his house. Steven ran to it enthusiastically, slamming his front door closed behind him.

"Best Western Hotel on Mathis Avenue," he demanded from the Uber driver, getting into the rear of the vehicle and leaning forward.

"Yes, I have the destination," the driver replied with a puzzled tone in his voice. He could tell Steven was in a hurry.

The Uber stopped outside of the hotel and Steven got out. As it drove off, Steven looked around to see if he could see Joanne, but couldn't spot her. Should he call her cellphone? Would that make him look too eager? He looked down at his cellphone and the screen showed 7:49. Maybe he was too early?

He stood there looking up and down the parking lot of the hotel. There was a woman standing a short distance from the hotel's entrance, wearing a long coat and holding a large gym bag, but it was not Joanne and Steven couldn't see anyone else. Maybe she was inside the hotel? Maybe he should ask at reception? he thought. No, he decided. He would wait until 8:00 p.m. before doing anything else.

He started to browse Twitter on his cellphone, then there was a tap on his shoulder. He looked up. The woman with the gym bag was standing there. Now that she was closer to him, he could see that she had long red hair that covered a lot of her face. She had on a long black coat and was also wearing sunglasses, even though it was dark outside. Steven said nothing for a second.

"Yes?" he then said. The woman brushed the hair away from her face.

"Joanne! I didn't recognize you, why are you dressed like that?"

"It's all part of the surprise," Joanne replied in a giggly voice. She opened her coat wide and he could see the sexy

French maid's outfit she was wearing beneath it, minus its white apron. Then she unzipped the gym bag and showed him its contents. Inside was a large tub of cookie-dough ice cream, his favorite; a tube of paint-on body chocolate; the white apron part of the French maid's outfit; and below all of those was a small backpack that was zipped closed.

"Wow," Steven gasped. This was going to be better than he had hoped for. Joanne led him by the hand into the hotel and to the room she had booked earlier via the internet.

She stopped outside the hotel room door.

"Uh-uh," she said, waving a gloved finger from side to side, "you can't claim your surprise without your claim card. I hope you didn't forget it?" Steven gave her a grin.

"No, I did not," he said and retrieved the card with the message on it from his back pants pocket. It was still in its envelope. He handed it to Joanne.

"Then you may enter," she said. She placed the card and its envelope into a side pocket on the gym bag and retrieved a room key card from the same pocket. Unlocking the door with it, she led him into the hotel room.

Once inside, she put the 'Do not disturb' sign over the outer door handle and locked the door behind them. "Take your clothes off," Joanne said in a slow and seductive voice, and Steven took them off so fast that it was fortunate he didn't rip any of his new clothing. "Now lie down," she said and pointed to the bed. He jumped onto it and spread himself facing her. The grin on his face was from ear to ear.

Joanne unzipped the gym bag and tipped the contents out. The ice cream tub, body chocolate, maid's apron, and backpack fell onto the floor. She took a moment to right the ice cream tub and backpack, then dropped her coat to the floor. Bending over, she partially unzipped the backpack, making sure Steven got a good view of her naked buttocks and thong. From the backpack, Joanne retrieved two pairs of long, furry, thick-chained handcuffs and two pairs of heavy-duty leather straps with buckles on them. Steven could not believe what he was seeing. Joanne had never been this kinky before. Early on in their relationship, they seemed to get on perfectly and their sexual chemistry was great as far as Steven was concerned, but since starting her new job, Steven had noticed that Joanne had become more and more distant and withdrawn, which had caused them to argue.

Now, Steven laid there naked and grinning. "Are you going to be a good boy and behave for me?" Joanne teased, and he nodded. She proceeded to cuff his hands to the headboard posts at the top of the bed. Steven was now sat on the bed with his back against the headboard and his arms splayed apart. Joanne then attached the leather straps, one to each of Steven's ankles, and buckled them tight. Steven sat, watching with awe, anticipation, and a little surprise, as this new, revived, kinky Joanne secured him to the bed. When she was finished, Joanne returned to the backpack, bent over again and fished around inside it. This time she retrieved two long thick chains. Each had a steel, load-bearing carabiner D-ring at one end, a common piece of mountain climbing equipment.

Steven continued to watch Joanne, his penis now fully erect, as she looped the chains around the bed's bottom legs and used the carabiner D-rings to secure them to metal loops on each of his ankle straps. She passed the D-rings through exactly the right loops in the chains to ensure his legs were pulled taut against the bed.

Joanne then went over to the pile of clothes Steven had left on the floor after he had stripped naked. She crouched down and began to rummage through them until she found his cellphone in his pants pocket and retrieved it.

"What are you doing?" Steven asked curiously. Joanne walked to the head of the bed, grabbed Steven's right thumb, and pressed it against his cellphone before he could work out what she was doing. She knew he unlocked his phone with its fingerprint scanner, she had seen him do it many times. The phone unlocked first time.

"Hey?" Steven said, a little puzzled. Joanne had been

quite rough in grabbing and placing his thumb onto the cellphone, and he thought she was maybe taking her kinky game a little too far.

She removed a glove, placing it onto a bedside cabinet, and tapped and swiped on his cellphone's screen before turning the screen to face him.

"Do you remember these?" she said. Steven looked at the screen. On it was displayed the cellphone's video and photo gallery app. Joanne had scrolled to the point in the gallery that displayed the video preview thumbnails of the homemade porn videos they had previously made.

"Mmmm." Steven gave a closed-lipped moan of approval. "Yes, I do," he said and smiled.

"Did you think it was funny when you made me record these? And now you threaten to send them to my parents, post them on the internet and show them to your friends?" Steven laughed.

"What are you talking about?" he said. "It was your idea to record those videos." Steven paused for a second before continuing to speak. "Oh, I get it, I'm a bad boy and you're the French maid that's going to punish me?" He smiled again.

Joanne deleted the videos, holding the phone in such a way so that Steven could see what she was doing. "Hey, come on!" he protested. "Why did you do that? Those were great."

"I want to tell you a story," Joanne said. "When I was 15, I fell in love with a boy named Peter Feldman. I trusted him, but he used me. He took inappropriate photos of me on his phone and then showed them to all of his friends. Everyone made fun of me for weeks after that, until I had a mental breakdown and had to be sent to see a therapist.

"About six weeks after my breakdown, I remember it was a Sunday, I was walking to a local store to buy a Slushie and I saw Peter riding his bike.

"He lived in the same neighborhood as me. He saw me and came over and spoke to me as if nothing had ever happened. He had no idea what he had put me through. I thought back to what my therapist, Dr. Ramsden, had taught me, about incorporating 'the shadow', so I acted like nothing was wrong as we stood there. We spoke for a while, and then he told me that he and his friends had made a camp in the woods behind his house and he'd show me if I wanted to see it.

"That's when I got the idea. I wasn't exactly sure how I'd do it, but I agreed to go with him to his camp. It wasn't far, and when we got there, there was an old sofa and a tree stump being used as a table with empty soda cans on it, in a small clearing.

"One of the trees there had a rope hanging from it. Peter boasted that he could climb into that tree in under ten seconds and I said, 'okay then, show me.' He wasn't lying, he climbed up that rope and into that tree pretty fast. I told him to stay there and let me climb up too. It took me a lot longer than him, and he laughed at me as I struggled, but I finally got into that tree. I asked him to move over and we sat next to each other on a thick branch.

"That's when I told him he could put his hand down my pants, into my underwear and touch me, just like he had always wanted to do. He looked surprised for a second but didn't hesitate. As soon as his hand reached the top of my pants, I held onto the tree trunk with one arm and pushed him as hard as I could with the other. He tried to stop himself from falling by grabbing the branch we were sitting on with his other hand, but that only made him pivot and fall from the tree headfirst. I heard his neck snap as his head hit the ground. I had incorporated my shadow, I had unleashed my demons and it was the best feeling I have ever had."

Joanne stopped speaking and smiled at Steven. Steven looked like he was about to say something but Joanne began to speak again.

"I climbed back down the tree and retrieved his cellphone from his pants. I knew his pin code, just like I know how you unlock your phone. I had seen him do it many times. I unlocked his phone and sent a text message to his friends, the ones that had enjoyed teasing me so much after Peter had shown them those photos of me.

"In the text message, I pretended to be Peter and told them that I was hanging out at the camp with my bike, and that they should come over if they weren't busy. Jordan Merriman replied almost right away. I thought it would be fitting for his friends to find him there, dead, at the bottom of that tree. Since they liked those photos of me so much, I would leave them with an image they'd never forget."

Steven looked confused and said nothing for a moment.

"Joanne," he said finally, "this is getting kind of weird and boring, and you're freaking me out a little. I'm not sure I like this anymore." He no longer had an erection and he felt a little spooked, but he reassured himself that what Joanne had just said was part of her dominant French maid act.

"Okay," Joanne said and smiled. "Don't worry, I have just the thing to make it better."

She put her glove back on and switched on the hotel room's TV, which was mounted to the wall. Then she picked up the TV remote and clicked through the channels until she found a music channel. She began to dance, and danced her way over to where the tub of ice cream and apron were on the floor. Still dancing, she put on the apron and got a spoon out of the backpack. With the spoon and the tub of ice cream in hand, she danced her way to the bed, climbed onto it and sat on Steven's lap. Then she took the lid off the ice cream tub and threw it to the floor. "Close your eyes and open wide. I'm going to feed you your favorite." Steven was a little hesitant but did as he was told. *Okay*, he thought, *now we're getting somewhere.*

Joanne reached into the ice cream tub and pulled out a leather gag that had a large plastic ball at its center. She put the ball part into his mouth and strapped the gag tight around his head as fast as she could, and it was fast because she had been rehearsing it. Steven opened his eyes, almost choking. He had a bewildered look on his face.

"Hmmmm hmmm hmm," came Steven's voice. It was impossible to understand what he was trying to say. Joanne got off of his lap and returned to the backpack, bent down and pulled out a small rectangular wooden cutting board, a large hammer, four three-inch nails, and a long, thick piece of rope. She then stood up and turned to face him.

"It was me that slashed your car tires," she said with a grin. The look on his face turned from puzzlement to terror. "HMMMM!! HMMMM!" came his muffled voice, this time significantly louder than before.

"Guess what I'm going to do?" Joanne said in a cold and sadistic voice, her face still holding a big smile.

"HMMMMMMMMMMMMM!" Steven screamed as loud as the gag would allow. He was struggling and yanking on the chains as hard as he could. His motion resembled that of a horse bucking. Joanne took the length of rope and passed it under the bed and then over Steven's waist. She tightened it as much as she could. She used a series of knots in the rope so that Steven's undulations would not loosen it. Now Steven's body was held quite tightly against the bed. Steven was still struggling and trying to scream but now his movements were restricted and any sound he made was masked by the music playing on the TV.

Joanne placed the cutting board under Steven's testicles and buttocks and positioned one of the nails over his testicles. It was difficult for her to line up while he struggled, but when she saw an alignment, she smashed the hammer down. The nail went through his scrotum and into the cutting board. Specks of blood spat over her white maid's apron. Steven was screaming, although his screams could not be heard. His eyes now looked bloodshot and there were tears running down his cheeks. Joanne felt the same warm happy glow she had felt when she heard Peter's neck snap. It was a feeling she had been longing for. She continued hitting the nail until it had passed right through the cutting board and then into the mattress.

She picked up a second nail from behind her on the bed, timed her strike and smashed it so that it too went through Steven's scrotum. More blood sprayed over her apron. Steven suddenly lost consciousness and stopped struggling. Joanne picked up a third nail and punched it through the head of his penis and into the cutting board.

"I have a right to be angry, I have a right to be aggressive," she said to herself, under her breath, and smiled.

Steven wasn't moving. She picked up a fourth nail and positioned it above his heart and raised the hammer. "I incorporate my shadow," she said out loud. "I have a right."

After a few moments of enjoying the feeling that the act she had just carried out gave her, Joanne stripped to her underwear. From the backpack, she removed the nurse's uniform, brown wig, another pair of gloves and a sheet of paper with telephone numbers written on it. She put on the new uniform, wig and gloves, then wiped any fingerprints off of Steven's cellphone and used his limp right hand to re-apply his fingerprints to it and the sheet of paper. She folded the sheet of paper several times and placed it into his pants pocket along with his cellphone. The sheet of paper was a list of phone numbers for local prostitutes and escort agencies Joanne had found on the internet.

Joanne had become quite good at finding things out from the internet. After Dr. Ramsden had helped her get her confidence back and explained the concept of 'the shadow' to her, she had used the internet to find out more about it. This took her down all sorts of rabbit-holes. For example, she learned how to buy stolen credit card information, where the card was still active. That's how she had paid for the hotel room she was now standing in. She learned to write in different styles of handwriting that would be hard to link to her actual handwriting style. She also found out how to use a voice changer and how to carry out caller ID spoofing: calling someone and making it look as though the call was coming from a different number.

Joanne put on her coat and sunglasses. She picked up the hammer, ice cream tub, red wig, maid's outfit, and backpack and placed them all into the gym bag, then put the gym bag over her shoulder. She unlocked the hotel room door and left.

"Now for Robert," she said to herself and smiled.

It was 9:12 p.m. when someone pressed Robert's front doorbell. *That's odd,* Robert thought, *who could it be at this time in the evening?* He went to the door and opened it. Standing there was a woman with long brown hair, in what appeared to be a nurse's uniform. She was wearing sunglasses and had a small backpack held over one shoulder. Her other arm was by her side.

"Yes?" Robert said when the woman didn't speak.

"Robert," Joanne replied.

"Joanne, is that you? Why are you dressed like that?" Robert said with some confusion in his voice.

"Robert, you know those phone calls you've been receiving? It's me. I'm the person that's been calling you," she said, holding a knife firmly in the hand by her side. She held it so that its blade was behind her leg where Robert wouldn't be able to see it. She was expecting him to be angry and shout at her, but he didn't.

"But why?" he said calmly, which she was not expecting. Joanne looked at him. He was handsome, she thought. He looked a bit like Dr. Ramsden.

"Because of what happened on Wednesday at work. Why did you turn me down when I asked you if you wanted to come out for a drink with me?"

"Oh," Robert said, and paused for a second. He looked a little embarrassed. "Listen, Joanne, you are a sweet girl, but technically you're young enough to be my daughter."

"So you think I'm ugly, is that it?" Joanne replied with a sadness in her voice.

"No, god no, you're gorgeous, it's just that…" Robert

was saying, but Joanne interrupted him.

"It's just what? I know you're single and I'm 19. If you really think I'm gorgeous then invite me in, see how we get on, and if you decide we don't get on, we don't have to take it any further." Joanne removed her sunglasses and hooked them into the neck opening of her top. Robert said nothing for a while. She was very attractive, he thought. She was the one approaching him, he wasn't doing anything wrong, and she was right, he was currently single.

"How do you know I'm single?" he then realized.

"I could tell you were single the first time I saw you at work," Joanne said, which was a lie; in actual fact, she had been stalking him. "So, are you going to invite me in?"

Robert said nothing for a couple of seconds.

"Okay, sure, come in," he agreed. "Follow me, I was only watching TV anyway," and he turned to lead Joanne into his house. Joanne took the opportunity, while his back was turned toward her, to throw the knife she was holding into some bushes on the perimeter of his front lawn.

Joanne entered the house and Robert closed the front door behind her. "Why are you wearing a nurse's uniform?" he asked as he showed her to his living room. She placed her backpack onto the floor and they sat down next to each other on his sofa.

"Oh, I'm a part-time trainee nurse," she said, lying, "and now that there's no work at the paint factory, I thought I'd do extra training to add towards my experience."

"I didn't know they trained nurses like that," Robert said, and then his face changed to give an expression of recalling something. "Oh, and about the factory. I'm not supposed to tell you this, but I got a call earlier from Morrison, one of the top guys at Chameleon Paints. He said that the explosion at the factory... You know there was an explosion, right?" Joanne nodded. "Well, he said that it looks like someone sabotaged one of the air compressors at some point before the weekend. I could have been killed.

Those compressors are next to my work area. Anyway, now I have to go to a meeting tomorrow with Morrison and some investigators."

"Oh, I'm sorry, that's terrible, I'm glad you weren't hurt."

"It's not your fault," Robert said, "you didn't sabotage the compressor."

Joanne looked blank for a second and said nothing.

"Are you okay?" Robert said into the silence, before Joanne leaned forward and began to passionately kiss him. Robert gave a hint of resistance for a second, but then gave in to her. After a few moments of kissing and caressing, Joanne stood up and took one of Robert's hands in her own.

"Take me to your bedroom," she said and smiled at him. Robert stood up and kissed her on her lips, then led her by the hand to his room.

"You know," Joanne said, "I like you a lot, Robert. Sexually, we can do anything you'd like. You can even take photos and record me, if you want to?"

4 DEBUG

They pulled their parachute cords within a few seconds of each other, each controlling their steering lines as they approached the ground. They had special lights attached to their legs, pointing downward, and controlled whether these were on or off with a button attached to one of the steering handles. These helped illuminate the ground as they got closer to it. Specially made altimeters gave a beep in decreasing intervals into their earpieces. Descending in the dead of night, they had to hope that nothing unexpected, such as a building or a tree, would suddenly appear beneath them.

Ezra landed first, smoothly, and Modal about 15 seconds later, a little harder and about 65 feet away. They had arrived in a field with vegetation between shin and knee height. Ezra unclipped herself from the parachute. She pulled a flashlight out of a pouch in her one-piece suit and double flashed it in the direction she thought Modal had landed. A double flash came back slightly to the left of where she thought he was. She walked slowly towards him in the darkness until she found him.

"That wasn't so bad," Modal said to Ezra as she came

and stood by him, her flashlight pointing at the ground to give them some visibility.

"Something isn't right," she replied. "The light patterns during descent were not correct. I think we are off-target."

"All things considered, being a little off-target is the least of our problems, we need to get out of this field," Modal said.

"Hold on," Ezra replied and pulled a device out of a pocket. She tapped on its screen, then slowly waved it back and forth above her head against the sky before looking at its screen again. "That doesn't make sense. I think we are way off-target."

"Let's just get out of this field," Modal said.

"Okay, gather your canopy and stay as close to this spot as possible. I'll go gather mine then come back to you and we can head towards those lights over there," Ezra said, pointing her flashlight towards some lights off in the distance.

Ezra and Modal stepped out of the field onto a country road close to a street light.

"Let's get out of these suits, take what we need and burn the rest," Ezra said. Modal nodded. A few minutes later they were out of the suits they had arrived in and each had a backpack over one shoulder. There were a couple of backpacks on the ground in front of them. Ezra bent down, picked up a small rectangular metal can from the ground, and popped the cap off of its pointed nozzle. She squeezed hard on the thin metal sides so that a stream of clear liquid came out and poured over the two backpacks on the ground. "Light it up," she said turning to look at Modal. He flicked something from his hand on to the liquid-soaked backpacks and they caught ablaze.

"Let's get out of here," Ezra whispered. They turned and began to walk up the road towards brighter lights further off on the horizon.

The sky began to lighten as sunrise approached the horizon. Ezra and Modal neared what appeared to be a small town or village on foot.

"Look at that," Modal said, pointing to a sign at the side of the road. It read, "WOLFISHEIM". "And that, and that," he added, pointing out other signs which looked like advertisements. "Those are not in English and I've never heard of a place called Wolfisheim. I don't think we are in the US, maybe in French Canada or something."

"Maybe…" Ezra replied. "Let's just go into the village and try and work out where we are. Maybe find a hotel."

They wandered the narrow streets of the small town as the sun dawned until they saw a middle-aged lady walking towards them.

"Excuse me, Ma'am, we are looking for a hotel. Do you know where we can find one? Can you direct us to a hotel?" Ezra said, approaching her. The woman stopped walking. She said nothing but looked Ezra and Modal up and down with a slightly curious and bemused expression on her face. "Ho-tel?" Ezra repeated. The woman said something that Ezra assumed was in French and then turned to point at a timber-framed building a little way down the road, similar in style to the rest of the buildings around them.

"Ho-tel," she added, pointing again.

They entered the doorway of the building the woman had pointed out. There were no obvious signs from the outside that this was a hotel, but upon entering they saw a magazine rack with papers and magazines in it next to a small reception area, and a woman sat in a chair asleep behind the counter.

"Excuse me," Ezra said. She did not press the bell that was on the counter. The woman behind the counter woke up a little startled and then stood up and began to speak in French. "I'm sorry," Ezra interrupted, "do you speak English?" The woman stopped speaking and appeared to look them up and down for a second. Modal lifted a newspaper out of the magazine stand.

"Yes, a little, can I help you?" she then said in a strong French accent.

"You need to look at this!" Modal whispered sternly into Ezra's ear.

"Hold on." Ezra shot a look back at Modal before turning her attention back to the woman behind the counter. "How much for a room?"

"It will be 65 euros a night," the woman replied.

"Euros?" Ezra said in surprise. The woman gave them a surprised look back.

"You need to look at this right now!" Modal whispered sternly into Ezra's ear and tugged slightly on her arm. "Excuse me, ma'am, can you give us a minute?" he said to the counter clerk and bustled Ezra out through the doorway and back onto the street.

"We are not in Canada, we're in France and it's not 1975, it's only 2014! We haven't traveled back far enough!" Modal said, shoving the newspaper he had taken from the magazine stand into Ezra's face. "We are totally fucked!"

Ezra said nothing for a while. "We're not just off target, we are nowhere near it in any sense," Modal continued. "It's a miracle the portal didn't open above an ocean, or so far up in the atmosphere we didn't instantly freeze or suffocate! Heck, 2000 and fucking 14, how is that even possible? It's a miracle the portal didn't open somewhere out in space. Well, it's game over man, it's game over."

"Shut up," Ezra finally replied. Modal was so caught up in his rant, he hadn't noticed that Ezra had retrieved the device she had used earlier when they had landed and was tapping on its screen. From appearances, it looked very much like a smartphone. After a while, she spoke.

"I know exactly where and when we passed through the portal, relative to where we are now. I just need to find our exact location on a map and our current time as accurately as possible. I can then use that, with the location of where the portal was meant to open, to get the G-Comp 4," she held up the device to indicate it, "to compute where Command will open the return portal for us in two days' time. We could still make it back." Modal went quiet for a second.

"Okay," he said, "what about the mission?"

"I don't know what to do about that yet," Ezra replied.

"Do you have a rough calculation as to where the return portal will open?" Modal said. Ezra tapped on her G-Comp 4.

"Well, somewhere in the eastern hemisphere. I mean, I don't know the current time or our current location so..." Ezra was saying but Modal cut her off.

"Somewhere in the eastern hemisphere! Are you serious! That's not going to help us. Even if we narrow down the location of the return portal, in case you forgot, we brought American passports 30 years out of date and 30,000 dollars in 1974 series 100-dollar bills. The money is most likely not valid in 2014, I doubt we can exchange it at a bank in France without being arrested and I think the woman in the street and the hotel clerk were looking at us funny because our clothing is from the wrong era," Modal said. There were signs of defeat in his voice.

"We're not done yet," Ezra said. "Follow me."

"Where are we going?" Modal asked.

After wandering the narrow streets for a little while, Ezra and Modal were now sat on a bench outside of a jewelry store in the center of the small town.

"What are we doing here?" Modal asked.

"Waiting for that store to open," Ezra replied, pointing at it. Modal said nothing. Ezra was the senior officer out of the two of them, even though she was a little younger than him and her physical abilities were not as comprehensive. After sitting and waiting on the bench for over two hours, someone appeared from inside the store's glass door and flipped over a sign so that it read "OUVERT" toward the street. They then unlocked the door and headed back inside.

"Come on, let's go." Ezra stood up and Modal followed.

Upon entering the store, they saw an elderly man sat behind a counter. It was a small jewelry store, with an upside-down L-shaped glass display counter running around the room and display cabinets on the left and right walls. The cabinets had jewelry in them but there were also plenty of empty jewelry stands. Ezra approached the man and took her backpack off her shoulder. The man watched her as she reached into it and pulled out five 100-gram gold bars and put them on the counter.

"I want to sell these," Ezra said.

"Where did you get those?" Modal asked. Ezra didn't reply. The elderly man was saying something in French. He picked up one of the gold bars, looked at it and put it back on the counter. He said something else and then pushed the bars back towards Ezra.

"No. No. I want to sell. Sell. Yes? You understand? Please," Ezra said, a little tension showing in her voice. The elderly man turned his head to the back of the store, shouted something and then began talking in a loud voice as if talking to someone in the distance. A few seconds later, sound could be heard as of someone descending steps and a door at the back of the store opened. A young man, 18-20 with dark hair, stepped through and closed the door behind him. He looked a little disheveled as if he had only recently woken up. He instantly caught Ezra's gaze and held it for a second before speaking with the old man. He then turned to Ezra and said, in a French accent,

"Allo, how may I help you?"

"I want to sell these gold bars," Ezra said, pointing at the five bars on the glass counter. "They are 24 karat gold and 100 grams each." The young man turned and spoke to the elderly man for a while. They went back and forth with the elderly man's hands and arms becoming animated as he spoke. The young man turned back towards Ezra.

"My grandfather says that we do not buy gold and even if we did, we do not have enough money here to buy even one bar from you. The bars have no, erm, how you say, markers? Erm, markings, gold markings. Also, we cannot verify this is gold for certain here. We do not have chemicals here to test, we do not repair here anymore and we do not buy."

"Fuck," Ezra said under her breath. She grabbed the bars off the counter, shoved them into her backpack and stormed out of the store. Modal followed.

Ezra sat on the bench outside the store and stared at the ground. Modal sat beside her.

"Where did you get those?" Modal asked.

"Command knew their calculations were not perfect. Yes, they had run tests but time was up, we had to go through, they couldn't put it off anymore. They knew the entry portal might be off, both location-wise and temporally. Modeling showed a standard deviation of two years and 100 miles of latitude. The longitude was more, I don't remember why, but I do remember they could get a good fix on the altitude; something to do with the Earth's iron core. I have a background in science but I wasn't involved in any way for the calculations, or design, or any of that stuff. I work for Alpha division just like you.

"In the debriefings, they showed that the extreme outliers of the bell-curve were up to 150 years off entry target, and location-wise, the entry point could have been anywhere, with the exception of the altitude. That was pretty much pinned down. Command reasoned that if we arrived off-target and survived, gold would always be worth something. We could use it to survive even if we couldn't complete the mission. Just like the reason for bringing the passports. As well as us being able to use them as fake IDs, they were a backup, in case we couldn't get a light aircraft for you to fly us through the return portal and had to do something drastic with a commercial flight," Ezra explained in a somber tone.

"Why wasn't I told any of this!" Anger flared in Modal's voice. Ezra snapped her head towards him.

"It was 'need to know' and you didn't need to know!" she told him sternly. Just then the young man from the jewelry store exited it and approached them.

"Allo again," he said. "You are American? I love America, I want to go someday to America." He was looking only at Ezra, as if Modal wasn't even there. "I am Eric by the way." He put his hand against his chest to indicate himself. "Are those bars really gold?" he added.

"Yes, they are," Ezra replied.

"That is crazy. Americans are crazy. I love Americans. I like your clothes by the way, very cool." Eric was looking at Ezra's flared pants and her vibrantly colored shirt with its large collar. "I am sorry we could not buy your gold. I wish I could help," he added.

"Do you know anywhere we could sell the gold?" Ezra asked.

"Well, maybe in Strasbourg, but I do not think it will sell so quickly. It is not marked so you will get less for it and people will be suspicious, but if it is real then it can be done," Eric replied.

"We don't have a lot of time," Ezra said, half to herself and half to Eric. "Do you have a map we can look at?"

"A map? No, I do not think anyone uses maps, but you can use my phone or my computer, they are in my room. We live above the store. I live with my grandfather. I want to leave, but he is old and I don't want to leave him alone. He does not want to retire yet. I do not know why, we do not do much business but he loves his store," Eric explained.

"You have maps on your phone and computer?" Ezra asked. Eric looked puzzled.

"Yes of course. Google Maps. On the internet. What kind of map do you need?" Eric seemed unsure of what she meant. Modal leaned over and whispered into Ezra's ear.

"This is 2014, they have the internet: the precursor to the infonet. It's limited but it can be used as a map or to search for basic information."

"Eric," Ezra said, reaching her arm out and taking Eric's hand, "I'm Ezra and this is Modal." She gestured with her head towards Modal. "Will you let us use your computer?"

Eric was silent and his face flushed slightly red.

"Oui, yes," he said after a second. Ezra let go of his hand. "Let me just speak to my grandfather. I will be right back." Eric went back into the store while Ezra and Modal watched through the glass door, still sat on the bench. Eric seemed to be having an intense conversation with his grandfather. They were both gesticulating. Finally, Eric returned to the glass door, opened it and beckoned them in with his hand. Ezra and Modal got up, reentered the store and followed Eric to the back of the room, all the while being watched by Eric's grandfather who had a disapproving look on his face. The old man mumbled something under his breath as they passed him. They went into the door at the back and up some stairs.

Eric's room was large, with a bed in one corner and a desk with a computer on it in the opposite corner. There was a bookshelf with books on it, a wardrobe, and a set of drawers in the room. Some clothes lay on the floor and there were a couple of posters and a clock on the wall. The ceiling slanted at one end, seemingly due to the roof. It looked like a typical young man's room. Eric switched on his computer and sat at his desk. After a minute or so he typed in his password and moved the mouse pointer on the computer screen, clicking on the Windows start button.

"I used to have a laptop," he said, "but I lost it while traveling a couple of years ago. I have not bought a new one yet." He clicked on something on the 'All Programs' menu. "Here," he said, "this is Google Maps."

"Can you show us where we are on the map?" Ezra asked.

"Of course," Eric replied and zoomed the map in. "This here, this is this building." He pointed at a gray rectangle on the screen. "Do you want satellite view?" he asked Ezra, who was leaning over him looking at the screen.

"No," she said. "Is there a way to find out the latitude and longitude?

"Yes, you just click on it and it will show you." Eric moved the mouse pointer over the gray rectangle that was the building they were in and clicked on it with the mouse. A small box appeared at the bottom of the screen and showed two sets of numbers: 48.587114 and 7.666286. Ezra retrieved her G-Comp 4 and tapped on its screen. She then turned her head and looked at the clock on the wall.

"Is the time on the clock correct?" she asked Eric.

"Err, oui, yes," he said. He picked up his cellphone and clicked a button on it, and when its screen lit up, he turned it around to face Ezra. The time on his cellphone matched the time on the wall clock. Ezra again tapped on her G-Comp 4. She then turned to Modal and showed its screen to him. It showed a map region of southeast Asia with a large red translucent circle stretching from Kuala Lumpur in Malaysia to Bangkok in Thailand.

"That's a huge area," Modal said.

"It will get smaller, the G-Comp can only compute so fast," Ezra replied. She then turned back towards Eric. "Eric, can you help us sell the gold? Can you take us to Stratberg?"

Eric swiveled his office chair around to face her.

"Strasbourg," he corrected her. "I knew you Americans were crazy. Nothing ever happens in this village, and then two Americans come here and try to sell half a kilo of gold to my grandfather and now they want me to take them to Strasbourg." Eric stopped speaking for a moment. Ezra looked at him and he looked back at her. "Yes, of course I can take you to Strasbourg, this village is so boring anyway. But I do not think you will sell the gold so easily. Is it really gold?"

Ezra knelt down to be at a similar level to where Eric was sat in his chair. She grabbed both of his hands with hers and looked intensely at him.

"Yes, I promise you it is real gold," she said.

"Maybe I can buy one bar from you and then sell it later," Eric said in response after a short pause. "I will have to buy it from you at a lower rate because I don't know how much I can sell it for later. Let me look up the price of gold." He turned and typed onto his keyboard. "3,161 euros for one bar… I can buy it for 2,000 euros. I will send it to your bank account. I know it is a low…" Ezra interrupted him.

"I don't have a bank account," she said. Eric laughed.

"Crazy Americans, I cannot get so much cash from the bank with such short notice. I would need to order it and collect it maybe one day later."

"Can you look up anything on that computer of yours?" Modal then asked Eric.

"Well it depends what 'anything' is, but yes you can try," Eric replied.

"Can you look up where we can buy an IBM 5100 computer?" Modal said. Eric typed on to his keyboard again. He kept silent for a short while as he read what was on his screen.

"This computer?" he then said, pointing to an image on the screen. "That is a very old computer, it was made in 1975, it is probably worthless. You cannot buy that now, you will be lucky to find it in a museum."

"It is not a worthless computer," Modal said. "That is an invaluable piece of equipment. That model computer is unique in its abilities. It has a secret built-in function that can natively emulate programs both in BASIC for system/3 and in APL systems/370. After the outbreak, with so much information lost, we lost our ability to reverse engineer or, 'debug', certain types of code and with the timeout bug approaching and the outbreak still…" It was only then that Modal noticed that Ezra was glaring at him to shut up without actually saying it. Modal stopped speaking.

"Can you see if it is in any museum?" Ezra asked Eric, who typed on his keyboard and clicked with his mouse.

"Oh, look at that. Yes, they still have a working one in the University of Stuttgart computer museum in Germany. That is the closest one I could find."

"Stuttgart, Germany, how far away is that?" Ezra asked. Once again Eric typed on his keyboard and clicked on his mouse. After looking at the screen he said,

"It is 162 kilometers away from here, not impossibly far. About a two-hour drive from here."

"We won't be able to cross into Germany, we don't have valid passports remember?" Modal said, looking at Ezra.

"You don't have passports?" Eric said with puzzlement in his voice. "You don't need a passport to cross into Germany from France. What happened to your passports?"

"They were stolen," Ezra replied. "Why don't we need passports to cross into Germany?" Eric laughed.

"Because we are in the European Union. You Americans really are crazy, I am loving this."

"Would we need passports to go to," Ezra paused to look at her G-Comp. "Kuala Lumpur?" she finished, looking back up. Eric laughed again.

"Yes of course," he said.

Ezra grabbed Eric's hands once more.

"Eric, where can we get passports, there must be a way? Please help us."

Eric looked at her. He could tell her emotions were genuine.

"Well, I know someone in Strasbourg who may know someone who maybe can get you passports. I do not know if it is possible for certain, and if so what the quality of them will be like."

"Quality?" Ezra asked.

"Oui, the quality of the fake passports."

"Yes, right," Ezra said, "Let me think a minute." She kept silent for a few moments and stared at the floor. "Eric, this is what we need," she finally said, looking up at him.

"We need passports, then for you to take us to the University of Stuttgart computer museum. We need plane tickets from Stuttgart to Kuala Lumpur and then plane tickets from Kuala Lumpur to somewhere else, but I don't know where yet. I will give you all five bars of gold."

"I know you two have done something, you have robbed a bank or something," Eric said. "As long as you are not terrorists or have not killed someone."

"We are not terrorists and we haven't hurt anybody, I promise," Ezra said. She picked up her backpack from off of the floor where she had placed it and tipped it on to Eric's bed. 15,000 dollars fell out, banded together in a few bundles, along with the five small gold bars. "That's 15,000 dollars," she said. "It's old currency, 1974 series 100-dollar bills, you can keep that too. You might be able to exchange them slowly over time."

Eric said nothing for a moment. Modal walked over to the bed and tipped out the contents of his backpack on top.

"That is 15,000 more of the same type of dollars."

"Whoo," Eric said, and clapped his hands together. "I knew there was a reason I loved Americans. Okay, let me make some phone calls and start this crazy adventure."

Eric picked up his cellphone and called several different people from what Ezra and Modal could gather. They couldn't understand what he was saying but his voice varied from serious-sounding to humorous and laughing. After about fifteen minutes of being on his cellphone, he said "Wait here," again only looking at Ezra, and left the room. They heard him descend the stairs.

"Do you think we can trust him?" Modal asked Ezra.

"We don't have a choice but he seems like an okay kid," Ezra replied.

"He likes you, have you seen the way he looks at you?"

Ezra was about to say something in reply but before she could do so, their concentration was drawn to the loud muffled voices coming from the store below them. After a few moments, the voices stopped and they heard footsteps coming up the stairs. Eric reentered the room, picked one of the gold bars up off the bed, and put it into his pocket. He stuffed the other four bars and the bundles of money into Ezra's now empty backpack and kicked it under his bed.

"Okay, we can go," he said.

"Everything okay?" Ezra inquired.

"Me, I love Americans. My grandfather, not so much," Eric said with a smile. They then followed him down the stairs, past his annoyed-looking grandfather and out of the store. Eric led them to his car, which was parked on a narrow street close by, and they set off for Strasbourg.

They arrived in the center of Strasbourg after only about 15 minutes of driving. Eric spoke for most of the journey about his family and his time at university, how he had come to live with his grandfather and how this trip they were now embarking on was the most excitement he had had in a long time. Ezra and Modal just listened without reply. Now they were parked in a narrow street in the city, outside a building with a Baroque architectural style.

"Okay, we are here, come," Eric said, getting out of the car. Ezra and Modal followed. Eric pressed the 'No. 3' button on a buzzer box on the wall next to the entrance door of the building. After a few seconds, a buzzing sound came from the door and Eric pushed it open. They climbed the stairs to the third floor and Eric knocked on the only door on that level. It had a black number '3' at the center top of the door. A man opened the door about four inches and looked out. He was middle-aged and scruffy-looking.

"Eric?" he said in a strong French accent.

"Oui," Eric responded. The man opened the door fully and all three went inside before he closed it behind them. He looked Ezra and Modal up and down before he began speaking to Eric in French. After a short while, the man looked at Ezra and said. "Come, come," beckoning her with his hand. They all went into another room.

In this room, via translation from the man to Eric and then from Eric to Ezra and Modal, they were asked to stand against a plain wall where the man proceeded to take a photo of each of them with a digital camera. He then went over to a desk that had a laptop, a printer, and other items on it. There were a few surgical knives, nozzled bottles, tweezers, a lamp, a magnifying glass on an adjustable stand and other instruments whose purpose Ezra and Modal could not fathom. They watched as the man printed out the photos he had taken and proceeded to use a variety of the instruments on the desk to transfer and attach the photos to the two passports, one after the other. The process was slow and took about an hour. After it was done, he said something and handed them both to Eric. Eric opened them and looked at them in turn.

"You are now Anna Belossi," he said, handing Ezra an Italian passport. "And you are now Luca Koller," he added, giving Modal an Austrian passport. Ezra and Modal both inspected their new fake passports.

"Why are they from different countries?" Modal asked. Eric spoke to the middle-aged man before replying.

"Passports do not grow on trees, he works with what is available," Eric relayed and gave a shrug. The man then began talking to him again. In response, Eric pulled from his pocket the gold bar he had placed there earlier, showed it to the man and carried on talking. Suddenly the man's voice grew loud and angry. He grabbed Eric by the throat with one hand and pushed him up against a wall.

Modal reacted with a set of swift moves. He punched the man in the back right side kidney area and, as the man let go of Eric's throat, kicked him in the back of the knees, causing his legs to buckle. Modal then placed his right forearm around the man's throat and in a snap move pushed the man's head forward with his left hand, with such incredible force that it hit the wall in front of them with a loud thud. The man fell to the ground seemingly knocked unconscious.

Eric stared at Modal. "What have you done!" he said in a loud panicked voice.

"I stopped him attacking you. The appropriate response is, 'Thank you'. Why did he attack you?" Modal replied.

"He didn't like my offer to pay him with the gold bar. I told him we did not have cash for the passports." Eric was talking to Modal but looking at Ezra. "Merde! Let us get out of here," he said, placing the gold bar on the desk at which the man had been working.

After leaving the forger's apartment, Ezra asked Eric to take them to stores where they could buy new clothes and a small suitcase. Eric complied and paid with his bank card and now they were sat in his small white Peugeot car in their new clothes. Ezra was looking at the screen on her G-Comp. It was now 11:32 a.m. local time on the 6th of March 2014. After sitting in silence for a few minutes, Eric spoke.

"What do we do next?" he asked, his enthusiasm seemingly back after the incident with the forger.

"We need to buy plane tickets and go to the university in Stuttgart," Ezra replied.

"Okay," Eric said, and without asking any further questions, drove them to an internet cafe. There, under Ezra's instructions, they bought plane tickets using Eric's bank card for Anna Belossi and Luca Koller from Stuttgart to Kuala Lumpur via Amsterdam. The total flight time was 14 and a half hours. The flight was due to take off at 8:20 p.m. and land at 5:50 p.m. local time on the following day, due to the flight time and time difference.

"What about the second flight?" Modal asked Ezra.

"I don't know, it's tricky, it's calculating an area about 300 miles northeast of Kuala Lumpur," she said, looking down at the G-Comp 4. "The return port..." she began to say, but looked at Eric and stopped herself. "The return area," she continued, "is going to have a radius of about 20 miles but will only be about 1,000 feet thick and be at an altitude of 10,000 feet. Command will keep it open as long as they can, about nine hours before they run out of power to sustain it." She tapped onto the G-Comp again.

"Can you bring up a list of all flights leaving Kuala Lumpur from midnight local time on the 8th of March?" she asked Eric. He typed it into the keyboard of the internet cafe's computer and a list came up. "That one there," Ezra said, pointing at the screen, "buy us tickets on that flight, business class tickets right at the front. It will be traveling in the right direction after takeoff."

"This is getting expensive," Eric said. "Those gold bars better be real." Ezra collected the 'print your own' flight tickets from the internet cafe's printer. They left the cafe and got back into Eric's car. After stopping at a gas station to fill up, they set off for Stuttgart.

"Okay, I have worked it out," Eric said. Up until that point, they had been sitting silently during the drive. "You two are American spies. It is okay, I know you cannot confirm that, but when you complete your mission, you know, when you save the world and have to complete the report after, make sure you put down: without Eric Chant, you would have failed." Eric laughed to himself, turned on the car's radio and tuned it to a German radio station. Ezra and Modal looked at each other.

They arrived at Universitätstraße 38, Stuttgart, exactly how the map app on Eric's cellphone had directed them.

"How do you want to do this?" Ezra asked Modal.

"Leave it to me," Modal said, pulling a smartphone-like device of his own out of one of his pockets. It looked similar to Ezra's device but was smaller.

"No," Ezra said. "We might need it later, the Pulsinc is single use only."

"I know how it works. Fine." Modal handed the Pulsinc to Ezra. "Just wait here and be ready," he added as he exited the car. Ezra and Eric sat in silence as they watched Modal calmly walk across the university parking lot and enter the main university building.

"So which part of America are you from?" Eric said out of nowhere, which caught Ezra a little by surprise as her attention was focused on the university building's entrance. They had been sitting without speaking for some minutes.

"I was brought up in Augusta, Maine," she said, then paused a second. "It hasn't changed much from when I was a child."

"Is Modal your boyfriend?"

"Oh," Ezra replied. "No... no." She paused again. "We, we are just friends."

"Do you have a boyfriend back in America?" Eric seemed very interested in the matter.

"Well, no," Ezra said, "I don't really have time for that, my work is more important right now."

"What work do you do?"

"Erm... well..." Ezra began to say when she was interrupted by someone shouting in the distance.

"Start the vehicle! Start the vehicle!" Modal was running towards them, carrying something bulky in his arms. Eric started the car while Ezra pushed the door closest to her open and scooted over so as to make room for the awkwardly running Modal. She could see what looked like a security guard and a few students come out of the university building and chase after Modal. They were gaining on him and the guard was shouting something in German.

"Shit, he's not going to make it! Drive to him! Drive!" Ezra shouted at Eric. The car jolted forward and Eric accelerated towards Modal. Ezra used her leg and foot to keep the car door from closing due to the acceleration. Eric drove past Modal, narrowly missing him, and straight at the group chasing him. They darted out of the way and a couple of students fell to the ground. Eric pulled the steering wheel hard to the right. His car tires made a screeching sound as he turned the car around in a tight a semi-circle as he could. Ezra held on to the seat in front of her, trying not to fall out of the car while keeping its door open.

Eric drove at the security guard, who had now almost caught up with Modal, but he dived out of the way as soon as he became aware of the approaching vehicle. Eric then drove past Modal, again narrowly missing him, and slowed the car to a screeching, almost complete, stop. This caused him to inadvertently lean one hand on the dashboard, turning the car's radio on and setting it to maximum volume at the same time.

Modal half threw, half passed the contents of his arms to Ezra, who was now half leaning out of the car door with her arms out ready to receive it. She caught it awkwardly and a second later Modal dived into the open car door. Ezra was pushed onto her back on the car's rear seats; the contents of her arms ended up on her abdomen and Modal on top of that. Ezra let out a grunt with the weight while the start of "Wouldn't It Be Nice" by the Beach Boys played loudly in the car.

"Go!" Modal shouted. The car's tires squealed on the ground for a moment, and then they zoomed out of the university parking lot with one car door still open and music blaring out. Their getaway might not have been smooth, but they had acquired a working IBM 5100 computer made in 1975.

Eric, Ezra, and Modal sat in silence. They were in Eric's car in an alleyway in the small town of Filderstadt, just south of Stuttgart airport. It was a six-mile drive from the University of Stuttgart where they had just left. For the whole six-mile journey Ezra was convinced they would be caught by police, but so far, they hadn't been. The time on Eric's car dashboard read 16:39, 4:39 p.m. on a 12-hour clock. Eric was still in the driver's seat and Ezra and Modal in the rear seats with the IBM 5100 computer sat between them. Finally, Ezra spoke.

"That was incredibly stupid and dangerous," she said. "Someone could have been killed, what were you thinking driving at those people Eric?" She turned to face Modal and spoke in a loud whispering voice. "That was unprofessional, that was your plan, to just grab it and run? We need to be more sophisticated than that. The whole point of this, the only reason for any of this, our entire mission, is to obtain a working IBM 5100 computer and return with it! Without it, everything we do is pointless! We should have planned it better!"

"We got it, didn't we!" Modal replied in a hushed stern voice of his own. "None of this was part of the plan. We were meant to 'buy' one," he said, putting emphasis on the word 'buy'. "Now, we're just making it up as we go. We don't have time for sophisticated plans."

He turned to Eric. "For what it's worth kid, I think you did okay."

"When on an adventure in the company of a couple of crazy Americans and you are their getaway driver, you have to drive like a getaway driver, no?" Eric responded. Ezra gave him a look and was about to say something, but stopped.

"Please just drive us to the airport," she said.

They all got out of Eric's car at Stuttgart airport's passenger drop off zone. Modal transferred the computer from the back seats of Eric's car into the suitcase they had purchased earlier, which was now in the car's trunk. Ezra handed something to Eric.

"I forgot about these. Our passports weren't stolen, they were just... unusable. Please destroy them when you get a chance," she said.

Eric looked down at what she had placed in his hands: two American passports with green covers. He opened one and inside was a black and white photo of Ezra. Eric didn't ask anything about them.

"Okay," he said. Ezra then handed him a piece of paper folded several times. Back at the internet café, when she went to collect the 'print it yourself' plane tickets, she had found some paper and a pen on a counter and scribbled him a note.

"This is for you," she told him. "Promise you won't open it for 48 hours."

"I promise," Eric said, and put it in his pocket along with the two American passports. They looked at each other for a moment and Ezra gave Eric a hug and kissed him on the cheek.

"Thank you for everything," she said.

"Will I ever see you again?" Eric asked.

"It's entirely possible," Ezra replied, taking his hand. "Get home safe."

She let go of his hand, and she and Modal walked into the terminal building, Modal wheeling the small suitcase behind him. Eric watched them disappear through the automatic terminal doors and then got back into his car.

Ezra and Modal sat in the departure lounge at Kuala Lumpur airport. Their journey from Stuttgart to Amsterdam, then onward to Kuala Lumpur had been uneventful. Their forged passports didn't set off any alarms and the IBM 5100 computer in the suitcase they were carrying, along with the clothes they had arrived in, didn't raise too many concerns. Modal explained it away, both at Stuttgart and Amsterdam airport X-ray security, as a computer they were donating to a school in Kuala Lumpur for the charity work they did there. The devices they were carrying also passed security without problem, both having the appearance of a cellphone. They had passed through Malaysian airport security just as easily. Now Ezra had pulled out her G-Comp and was tapping on it.

"Everything okay?" Modal asked.

"Yes, I think so. The calculated return portal's position has stabilized to this location." Ezra turned the device's screen to face him.

"So, can I ask you something," Modal said. "How do we know the return portal will open at the right time? Since the entry portal we arrived through opened 40 years off-target, how do we know the return portal will open two days after the entry portal and not at some other time?"

"Well, Command will use exactly the same inputs they did when they opened the entry portal, only two days later from their perspective."

"If they are using exactly the same inputs, why doesn't the return portal appear in the same location as the entry portal?"

"The way it was explained to me is that, to put it simply, the Earth is moving. It's spinning, it orbits the sun and the sun is moving in our galaxy and so on. Time on the other hand, to an approximation, is moving at a constant rate, accounting for general relativity." Modal looked puzzled. "Basically, the time part of the calculations is easier to calculate than the location part. So, if Command's calculations had been perfect, the entry portal would have opened on the correct date in 1975 at the correct location and then two days later the return portal would have opened at the same location. The original error in the entry portal's location cascades onto the return portal's location, but the error in the entry portal's 'time' effectively doesn't. Command will open the return portal two days after they opened the entry portal from their frame of reference, and it will open two days after the entry portal opened from our frame of reference as well. Command knew there could be problems. That is why the return portal will be much, much larger than the entry portal and will stay open for as long as Command can sustain power to it, to give us a chance to find it. They keep all the inputs the same, just increase the power to make a bigger return portal. Command planned that on purpose in case the entry portal's location was off, and it was."

"More shit I should have been told about," Modal said in a disgruntled tone.

"I don't see what difference it would have made. Ultimately, we both knew this might be a one-way trip and even a one-way trip to death. You took the responsibility because you wanted it, not because they tricked you into it."

Modal sat in contemplation of that. "Look," Ezra then said, pointing at a flight departure information screen. It instructed them to go to departure gate C1 for flight MH370.

Modal and Ezra sat next to each other at the front of the plane in business class on Malaysia Airlines Flight 370, en route to Beijing. They mostly had business class to themselves. Once the 'fasten your seat belts' sign had gone out, Modal pulled the Pulsinc device out of his pocket. He clicked a button on it and a small compartment at the bottom opened up, from which four small black objects fell out into his hand. He passed two of them to Ezra. They both put one in each ear. Then they just sat and watched the cockpit cabin's door through a half-drawn curtain that separated the plane's forward area from the business class section.

After about 25 minutes they saw the cabin door open; either the pilot or co-pilot was taking a bathroom break. Modal immediately tapped on the Pulsinc and a pulse of some type shot through the aircraft in all directions. Everyone but Ezra and Modal fell unconscious. The two unclipped their seat belts, removed the objects from their ears and rushed to the front of the airplane. They opened the cockpit cabin's door fully and dragged out who they judged to be the co-pilot. Finally, they drew closed the curtains that separated the forward area, then went into the cockpit and locked the door behind themselves.

After about a minute the pilot came to. Ezra was sat in the co-pilot's seat and Modal was stood behind the pilot, pressing the rounded corner of the Pulsinc into the back of the man's head to give the impression that it was a weapon capable of firing a projectile.

"Don't turn around," Ezra said. "My colleague is behind you and you won't like what he will do to you if you don't do exactly what I say. Do you understand?" The pilot nodded. "Good, do what we say and no-one gets hurt. Fly to these coordinates and descend to 10,000 feet before we get there."

Suddenly there was a banging on the cabin door. The co-pilot had also come to and was trying to enter the cabin. "Tell him this is a hijacking and if he doesn't want anyone to get hurt, he will stop banging, not cause any problems, not alert the passengers and stay in the forward area behind the curtain." The pilot shouted something loudly in Malaysian over his shoulder and the banging stopped.

"Good," Ezra said. "Now announce to the passengers that there was a problem with the plane's air supply but everything is now 100% fixed and there is absolutely nothing to worry about. If any of them feel dizzy this will pass in a few minutes." The pilot made the announcement over the aircraft's intercom system in both English and Malaysian. "Good," Ezra said again. "Now turn off all of the plane's communication systems." The pilot did as he was instructed.

Some time had passed and Ezra kept checking the G-Comp, looking out of the windows and checking the plane's altimeter.

"Something is wrong," she said. "It's not here. We should be able to see it."

"What are we looking for?" Modal asked.

"It should look like a cloud that's being periodically lit up by lightning from the inside, only the lightning will be purple, vivid purple. To weather satellites, it will look like a storm cloud. It's 20 miles wide, we should easily be able to see it."

"Fuck," Modal said.

"Let me think, let me think!" Ezra replied, and began frantically tapping on her device.

"Shit," she finally said. "Malaysia doesn't use daylight savings time and the US won't change their clocks until the 9th of March. It's still the 7th there now. I made a stupid mistake." She tapped on the G-Comp again then showed its screen to Modal.

"We're fucked!" Modal said in response. The device's screen now showed a large red translucent circle off of the northwest coast of Australia. Ezra tapped on it again.

"Change the plane's heading to this and re-ascend to 35,000 feet," she said to the pilot, and showed him the G-Comp's screen. The pilot complied and the plane began to bank to the left. Ezra could sense Modal looking at her.

"The area will narrow by the time we get closer to the general region. Just like before," she told him. She could tell what he was thinking. Modal whispered into her ear.

"Are we going to get there in time before the portal closes, if it's even there? Does this plane have enough fuel to reach so far south?"

"I think it will be close on both counts," Ezra replied.

After approximately eight tense hours of flying, yellow warning lights were flashing on the plane's dashboard. The co-pilot had periodically been banging on the cockpit cabin's door. Ezra and Modal had ignored him. Finally, the pilot spoke.

"We are going to run out of fuel. Everyone will die, we need to change heading towards land, switch communications back on and declare an emergency right now!" he said. Ezra looked at the G-Comp's screen.

"Stay on this heading and descend to 10,000 feet. Do it now or everyone on this flight will die," she ordered. The pilot began the descent.

"There!" Modal said, pointing out of the cockpit windows. Below and in front of them was a huge oval-shaped cloud, stretching across the horizon, which appeared to be crackling and fizzing with electricity and strobing with purple lights.

Suddenly an audible alarm began to sound. It beeped twice and then a recording of a stern male voice said, "Warning! Low fuel," before the sequence repeated over. Ezra and Modal looked at each other.

Eric was sitting on his bed browsing the news on his cellphone when he read about Flight MH370 being declared missing. He instantly retrieved the note Ezra had handed him outside the departure terminal at Stuttgart Airport and opened it. The note read,

Dear Eric,

I hope you waited to open this note. If so, you have probably heard something about Flight MH370. If the plane crashed, then our mission has failed, we are dead, we are responsible for the deaths of the innocent people on that flight and humanity has a bleak future. The same is true if you hear we have been arrested in Beijing. If, however, you hear that the plane has disappeared without a trace, we may have succeeded. The people on that flight have been torn away from their families but are alive and well. Unfortunately, this is a necessary evil. Do not tell anyone about this for your own protection. This is not going to make sense to you, but in the year 2036, between February 3rd and February 18th, you should take a vacation within the borders of the USA and bring any loved ones along with you. Thank you for all of your help.

Ezra

5 KARMA EXTRA

It was 7:45 p.m. and Alan was leaning up against the wall outside of Club Paradise. He had on his best shirt, which was a horrid grey color, and made anyone who saw it think it had once been white. He also wore a pair of black pants and worn black shoes. He was in a bad mood after having had an argument with his wife about going out for the night, because despite the fact that he told everyone he was the boss in his relationship, quite the opposite was true. Alan looked down impatiently at his watch. It was now 7:49 p.m.

"Where the hell are they?" he said out loud to himself. Just then he heard a voice call out.

"Alan you bald dick, you're here," Simon said. He was walking towards Alan, still a little ways off, with Adam and Joe alongside him. All three of the new arrivals were Alan's work colleagues.

"Where the hell have you been?" Alan yelled back at them.

"Long story," Simon said. "Adam almost caused a fight with some other guys on the way here."

All four men entered the club and took up a table close to the large circular stage on which the girls performed their dances. Alan was already excited and could not wait for the shows to begin, but it was still too early for that as the performances started at 9:00 p.m. The reason they had arrived so early was to ensure themselves front row seats. Alan noticed that there were a surprising number of women seated in the place. He had thought that a place like this would only be full of men and that the only girls present would be on stage, but he was happy to be wrong. Simon bought the first round of drinks and they all settled down to talk about women, what they had done with them and what they wanted to do to them, typical men's banter.

As they sat talking, Alan felt someone sit at the table behind him. A few seconds later he felt a second person sit.

"Hi, I know you probably hear this all of the time but I'm just going to come out and say it anyway. I think you are absolutely stunning and so I was wondering if I could buy you a drink?" Alan overheard a voice say. He stopped listening to Joe going on about clitorises and was now eavesdropping on the conversation that had started up behind him.

"What?" questioned a female voice in response, a hint of confusion in her tone.

"Can I buy you a drink?" the male voice replied. Alan listened in closely but he didn't turn around; doing so would make it obvious he was listening.

"Err… Okay. Sure," she said after a short pause.

"Not here. Would you like to come back to my private bar and I'll pour you the drink myself?" the male voice said. After a very long pause, the woman replied.

"Yes."

Alan heard them both get up from their table and walk away. After a second or two, he turned and looked to see an attractive girl walking away with a man. He could only see the man's back, not his face. Alan watched as they left the strip club.

"Who are you perving on now Alan?" Simon inquired on seeing Alan's head turned away from their table.

"No, I thought I knew that guy from somewhere," Alan lied. What he was really thinking to himself was, *how the hell could a pick-up line like that work and why can't I have luck like that?* "You know what," he continued, turning to face his colleagues at the table, "Places like this won't exist soon, with all of these feminists taking over the world. Everything is politically incorrect nowadays. If a woman dresses like a whore, everyone knows she wants it, and if she doesn't enjoy the sex, or the guy doesn't call her back afterward, well, she just reports him for rape the next morning. Women have it too easy if you ask me and if they dress like whores, they deserve whatever happens to them. If you know what I mean?"

"Here's to the whores," Joe said and raised his beer bottle. The others followed suit, erupting into laughter.

Soon it was time for the dancing to begin and Alan rushed to the bar to get a round of drinks in before the dancers came onto the stage.

"Can I have four bottles of Bud?" he requested from the barman.

"What about a drink for me?" he heard a soft voice say and turned to see a gorgeous girl standing there. She was about 5'7" tall with long blonde hair, deep green, almond-shaped eyes and a large smile on her face. She was wearing tight black leather pants and a tight green top that revealed her belly button and the tops of her breasts. Alan was so shocked he said nothing for a while.

"Yes, yes... Yes... Yes... What... What would you like?" he finally managed to say.

"Do you have a car?" she said. The barman who was waiting to hear what drink she would choose turned to serve someone else on hearing this.

"Yes... I... It's... no... It's at home," Alan managed to babble.

"Well, I guess you can't take me back to my place then," she said in a slow seductive voice.

"No... No, wait... I can get us a taxi," Alan quickly

replied, for he may have been fat and old but he still had some wits about him. Maybe he wasn't past it after all, he thought, maybe this strip club was lucky, maybe girls came to this club to be picked up. The guy at the next table had walked off with an attractive girl, so why couldn't he?

"Do you want to call one and we can go back to my place?" she said, running her fingertip over her lips. Alan could not believe what was happening, this was too good to be true.

"Look… I… I don't want to be rude but…" he began to say, but the girl interrupted him.

"If you're about to ask me if I'm a prostitute, I am going to slap you and leave. I happen to find you attractive. If you don't find me attractive, say so and I will leave you alone," she said in a stern voice.

"No, I was going to say, this doesn't happen to me often," Alan replied, which was a complete lie as he had indeed been considering whether she was a prostitute and was about to ask that very question, albeit indirectly.

"Well, I find you very sexy. You remind me of my father," the girl said. Alan thought about that for a second and came to the conclusion that weird was acceptable but prostitute was not. Just as well, he thought, because had she been a prostitute, he probably couldn't afford her anyway.

"Let's go get that taxi," Alan said enthusiastically, totally forgetting about his work colleagues still sat at the table waiting for him to return with the round of drinks.

The taxi pulled up and Alan and the girl got out. Alan paid the driver, whose cost was quite substantial because they had been driving for quite a while, heading out of the city. They now appeared to be in an industrial park at the edge of a small town. The girl had given the taxi driver the directions and Alan hadn't been paying attention, so he wasn't at all sure where they were.

The taxi drove off and left the two of them standing there. Alan looked at the buildings in front of him. They were standing in front of one of the doors on a row of small business units. In fact, there weren't any other buildings close by. The next nearest buildings were some way down the road. The entire row of business units looked like they were in need of repair; the paint had come away from most of the shutters, doors and window frames.

"Shall we?" the girl said in a giggly voice, motioning her hand towards the door.

"You live here?" Alan asked.

"Oh, it's not as bad as it looks and it's very cheap. It's okay, you'll see," she replied.

"I just realized. I don't even know your name," Alan said.

"Forsinia."

"That's unusual, is it foreign?"

"No. Just something I chose for myself," she said, with a hint of 'so there' in her voice. Alan had already decided she was quirky and thought it best not to inquire any further, since he knew he hadn't come to this place with her to have an intellectual conversation—not that he himself was capable of one, so to speak.

Forsinia unlocked the door to the building and Alan followed her in. She locked and bolted the door behind them and flipped a light switch on. Alan looked around. They were in an old car workshop of some kind. There were old car parts lying around and high, empty racks of heavy-duty industrial shelving units along the side walls. The place looked like it hadn't been used in quite some time. Running along the back wall were what Alan judged to be a row of three glass partitioned offices, with the blinds drawn from the inside. "Don't worry. Come," Forsinia said soothingly. She flipped the light switch back off again and carefully led Alan by the hand in the dark to one of the offices. Alan couldn't help but feel a bit apprehensive and was also now noticing an odd smell, like wet paint.

Once inside the office, Forsinia flipped on another light switch. Alan was surprised to see that the office had been converted into a contemporary looking bedroom. On the back wall were mounted half a dozen red candles spaced equally apart. A large pink bed sat under the candles against the back wall and large, built-in wooden wardrobes ran down one side of the room. The floor was comprised of rustic floorboards and even had a pink rug on it. Alan wondered why someone had bothered to convert an office, in an old car workshop, into a bedroom.

"Now strip for me, slowly," she said in a seductive voice, pulling the sexiest pose she could manage. Alan slowly took his clothes off, first his shoes and socks, then his shirt, pants, and large, cream-colored, Y-front underpants, leaving them in a pile on the floor to reveal his pudgy body.

"I hear that it's very warm this time of year in FLORIDA," Forsinia said all of a sudden, saying the word 'Florida' particularly loudly.

"What?" Alan replied, somewhat puzzled. Then suddenly, and without warning, two large men jumped out of the built-in wardrobes. One appeared to be wearing a Batman costume and the other a Robin outfit. "What the fu…" Alan began to say, but before he could finish his sentence, the men pounced on him. They were very large and muscular and easily overpowered the bald and overweight Alan.

Forsinia kicked the pink rug so that it went under the bed, then crouched down and pulled at a brass ring that was attached to the floorboards. A portion of the floor slid under the bed to reveal four large black iron rings, bolted to more wooden floorboards below the sliding panel. Forsinia then retrieved four lengths of rope from the wardrobe, and she and the two men proceeded to tie Alan face down by his wrists and ankles to the iron rings.

Alan was struggling as vigorously as he could and shouting out at them. "Let me go you fucking freaks! What the hell are you doing! You untie me now or you'll all be fucking sorry!" Forsinia ignored Alan's cries and went to the wardrobe. She brought out a large roll of wide brown packaging tape and handed it to the man in the Batman outfit. Alan couldn't see any of what was going on behind him now. All he could see was the base of the bed and its pink covers draping down.

Forsinia calmly took her shoes off, then her pants and her tight little top and tossed them all onto the bed. Finally, she removed her panties and stepped over Alan's head so that she had one foot on either side of his ears. She crouched down, and as Alan continued to shout, stuffed her slightly damp panties into his mouth, which he was not expecting. Batman was ready with the packing tape and taped over his mouth immediately, looping it around his head a few times. Alan continued to try and shout, but all that could be heard now were soft muffled cries.

Forsinia returned to the wardrobe and brought out a large, strap-on rubber penis that must have been at least eight inches long and two inches in diameter, along with a tube of what was labeled 'Smooth fit gel'. She put on the strap-on, as if putting panties on, and fastened it tight around her waist with a buckle. She then squeezed the contents of the tube all over the large appendage protruding out from between her legs and rubbed the clear, gel-like substance all over it. Alan, unaware of what was taking place behind him, continued to struggle and try to shout for help.

Forsinia knelt down, one knee either side of his buttocks and placed the tip of the appendage between them.

"Who's the daddy?! Who's the daddy now you bitch?!" she began to shout as she started to force the fake penis inside Alan. Alan's body had never known so much pain; he felt like he was being torn apart. "You're my bitch now!" Forsinia laughed sadistically. "I'm going to force it in ya, because you're my bitch and I'm your daddy!" She continued shouting as she thrust her body forwards and back. Batman and Robin stood there and took up positions to get a good view of the action.

The appendage was now almost all the way inside Alan. Forsinia continued to thrust as hard as she could, and she was beginning to moan louder and louder. Alan felt as if his eyes were about to pop out of his head. His entire body ached and he thought he might pass out. The only thing he could think about, other than the pain he was in, was *why are these freaks doing this to me?*

After a short while, Forsinia let out a loud cry and stopped her thrusting. She pulled the appendage out slowly and stood up. "Okay, Yohan, you may now have your turn," she said to the man wearing the Batman outfit.

"Zank you mistress," he replied with a strong German accent and proceeded to lower his tight black leggings and assault the now sobbing Alan. When Batman was finished, Forsinia spoke again. "Okay, Hans, now you," she said, and in response, the man wearing the Robin outfit also acknowledged her in a strong German accent, then lowered his leggings and assaulted Alan for some time. There was nothing Alan could do but sob and hope it would soon be over.

When Hans had finished, Forsinia spoke once more. "Get dressed," she said, "We are going to go and get Olu so he can have his turn." The two German men went to the wardrobe and put on a change of clothes, as did Forsinia. Forsinia then removed Alan's wallet and cellphone from his pants, which were still lying on the floor. She switched off the light and the three left the room.

Alan lay there crying in the darkness for a minute or two, then managed to compose himself a little. He pulled and tugged at the ropes binding his wrists as hard as he could and they began to cut into him. He pulled and pulled and eventually freed his right hand from one of the ropes, at the cost of badly grazing his wrist and the lower part of his hand. He used his right hand to try and untie his left, but it was shaking and it took him some time.

Once he had both hands free, he unwrapped the packaging tape from his head, which caused him quite a bit of pain as it pulled away from his skin. It would have been a lot worse were it not for the fact that Alan was bald. He pulled the panties out of his mouth, gasping, and tossed them onto the floor. Then he pushed himself up onto his knees, crouched down and frantically tried to untie his ankles, for at least ten minutes had passed since Forsinia and her fellow assaulters had left, and Alan was beginning to worry that they might return with a fourth person now in their group.

Finally, he managed to undo the ropes around his ankles. He found the light switch and flipped it on, then scrambled over to his clothes and searched the pockets of his pants. Both his wallet and cellphone were gone. He put on his pants, shirt, and shoes without bothering about his underpants or socks.

Alan went from the room to the building's front entrance as fast as he could in the darkness. He stumbled around feeling the walls until he found the light switch and flipped it on. He desperately tried to open the door through which he had entered into the building, but it was locked. Next, he tried to open the large shutter that vehicles had presumably once used to enter the building; he could find no way to open it or any kind of control switch for it.

Alan searched, looking for something that might help, until he found a rusty crowbar. He wedged it between the door and its frame and began to push, putting his weight into it. The crowbar slipped awkwardly out of the gap between the door and its frame and Alan hurt his hand against the door, but he no longer cared about pain. He had to get out of there and kept trying to pry the door open. Again and again he pulled, jerked, and leaned on the crowbar, letting out a growl with each gyration.

The frame eventually buckled and the door popped open. Alan's hand was pulsing with pain. He dropped the crowbar and without doing up his shirt buttons, he headed out the industrial park as fast as he could manage and towards some lights a short way off in the distance.

Alan heard what sounded like a passenger plane flying

low overhead and stopped running to look up. The plane seemed to be descending in order to land somewhere relatively close by. Alan suddenly thought he knew where he was. He thought back to when Forsinia had spoken to the taxi driver and the name of the place she had told him to take them. It had been in the news on TV recently: a small town near the city's main airport was going to be demolished in order to facilitate the building of an extra runway. Alan remembered the news report explaining that, as people were slowly moving out, it was becoming more and more a ghost town. A reporter for the news channel had been interviewing a middle-aged man about how he felt about the government forcibly buying his property. The man had told the reporter that even though he was given a fair price for his property, he didn't want to move. This must be where he was, the airport ghost town from the news reports. Alan carried on heading towards the lights and buildings ahead of him.

Alan had now slowed to a walk and was slightly out of breath. He looked down at his watch; it was 12:03 a.m. The street lights which had drawn him in this direction illuminated the area, but it was only now he saw that the buildings were boarded up. He wandered along the road looking for someone that might be able to help him, or any signs of activity from any of the buildings. Then he saw movement coming from a building a little way down the road. As people passed in front of the windows, the intensity of light coming from them changed. It even looked as though a party was going on in there. Alan hurried over to the building and stopped outside. He couldn't see through the frosted windows, but he could hear music coming from inside.

Alan then heard another sound coming from behind him and turned to see a distant, dark-colored van drive into the industrial park area from where he had just come. On seeing this, he turned to face the doors again and burst inside.

"Please… Please… Can somebody help me, please? I've

been attacked!" Alan said. The music stopped dead and the place went silent. He was in some kind of makeshift bar or club that was full of men dressed in leather. Some had stud collars, others had leashes around their necks.

"Well look what we have here," said a tall, completely bald-headed man, approaching Alan.

"Please," Alan said, "I need help."

"I know how to help you," the man replied. Alan heard someone lock the door behind him and started to think the worst.

"I just need to make a call, I don't want to cause any trouble," Alan said. No-one replied and there was a moment of silence.

"I will be on my way," Alan then said. He turned to leave and saw two burly, leather-clad men barring his way.

"Mama's-Boy. Come here," the bald man said from behind Alan. Alan turned back around. A man wearing tight leather pants and a latex top, with cut-outs through which his pierced nipples showed, walked over to the completely bald man.

"Do you think this gentleman should be allowed to leave?" the bald man continued.

"No Rex, I don't," Mama's-Boy replied.

"What's going on?" Alan said with panic in his voice.

"We're about to have us some fun is what's going on," Rex said, grinning at Alan, and snapped his fingers. Four large men grabbed Alan, two by each shoulder and two by the upper arms, and the whole bar erupted in cheers. One man swiped a table clear with his arm, knocking bottles and other things onto the floor, and then dragged it over to where Alan stood struggling. Then the four men holding Alan forced him to bend over the table and Rex pulled his pants down. "Wow! Would you look at this!" Rex shouted, gesturing at Alan's buttocks. "This one is ready to go!"

"No, please! No! NO! NO! PLEASE!" Alan began to scream, unable to believe what was happening to him again. Just then there was a loud rapping at the door.

"Shit! Police!" someone shouted, and the atmosphere turned to panic with men running all over the place. In the chaos, Rex and the four men who had been holding Alan down ran to the door as if to barricade it. Alan did not hesitate. He pulled up his pants and pushed his way past the masses of leather-bound men to the back of the room. He found a door with a round glass window in it and went through, finding himself in a small corridor. A door to his left read 'Gentlemen', and a door to his right had the word 'Ladies' crossed out and red graffiti scrawled below it that read 'More Gentlemen'.

Alan looked back through the small circular glass window into the room from which he had come. He was hoping that the police were about to burst into the makeshift bar. He looked and listened intently and saw the commotion in the room suddenly die down. Rex slowly opened the building's entrance door. Standing there was Forsinia, with two large white men and a large black man that Alan guessed were Hans, Yohan, and Olu.

Alan could not see very well or hear what was being said, but Rex seemed to recognize her and he was pointing to the back of the bar. Alan turned, ran in through the door labeled 'Gentlemen', and bolted the door behind him. Inside was a room with a single toilet. He climbed up on the toilet and frantically tried to open the small window on the back wall above it. Because the window frame had been painted while the window was closed, it was difficult for Alan to open, but he knew he didn't have a choice; he would rather die than go through that again. He pulled on the handle as hard as he could, and the pain in his right hand from earlier amplified tenfold, but the window finally gave way and reluctantly jerked open. It was a very small window and as he dragged himself through, he ripped his shirt and grazed his shoulders, arms, stomach, and back. He landed on the ground outside with a thud, but quickly picked himself up.

Now he was in a small alleyway running along the back

of the buildings. One direction led to a dead-end and the other to a road. He was sure he could hear a thudding sound coming from inside the window he had just climbed out from. Someone was trying to break open the toilet door.

Then Alan saw a black metal fire-escape on a building opposite the one he had just exited. The metal staircase ran the entire height of the building, with a fire-escape door leading to it from every floor. He ran to it, breathing heavily, and tried to push open the ground floor door but it held firm and refused to open. He ran up the first flight of metal steps and tried the fire-escape door on that floor. It opened right away, and Alan hurried inside and shut it behind him.

Alan found himself in a corridor with six doors, three on each side. The doors were numbered 1 to 6 and two of the doors had 'Do not disturb' signs over the doorknobs. Alan guessed that he was in a hotel of some kind. He hadn't noticed a hotel from the street. He walked over to the nearest door, number 5, and knocked but there was no reply. He had to get to a phone and call the police, he thought to himself. He turned to face door number 6. Alan saw the 'Do not disturb' sign over the handle, but that was the least of his worries. He knocked on the door, and again there was no answer, so he tried the handle. He no longer cared who was inside or what they might say. He just wanted to get out of the corridor in case Forsinia and her friends had seen him enter the hotel from the fire-escape. He was desperate to call the police.

The door was not locked and it opened. Alan quietly walked in and closed the door behind him. He was in a short corridor that led to a room. There was a door on his left and dim lamplight appeared to be coming from the room ahead of him. From his position in the corridor, all that Alan could see in the room ahead was a desk with a TV above it, mounted to the wall. Then he heard a moaning sound, followed by a woman's voice saying,

"Yes! Yes! Ride me you stallion, ride me! Show me your

stallion-ness! I am a wild mare! Tame me you stallion, tame me! YES! YES! Harder! More!"

Now Alan knew what that 'Do not disturb' sign was for, and possibly why no-one in this room had responded to his knocking. He decided he would just have to interrupt them and ask to use their phone. It was either that or go back out and try to find another phone.

Slowly, Alan walked into the room. Facing away from him was a naked woman on her hands and knees on the bed, and a naked man behind her with his hands on her hips. It seemed as if he was keeping still and she was thrusting backward into him. "How's my little stallion doing? Is he going to be a good boy and satisfy his mare! Ride me! Ride me like a stallion," continued her moaning voice.

"Excuse me," Alan said. The woman let out a yell.

"Aghhh! Who the fuck are you?" she said, turning to face him with a single jump and spin motion as did the man. The woman was much older than the man, who looked to be in his late teens. She hid behind him and tried to cover her breasts with her forearm.

"Please, you have to help me," Alan began to say, "I've been attacked, these crazy people..." but he was interrupted as a loud thud shook the paper-thin walls of the cheap and grimy hotel. Then muffled voices could be heard.

"Hey man, what's going on... No-one's hiding in my room! Hey those are my clothes!" came the distant voice of a man, mixed in with other less clear voices from somewhere within the building. 'Thud!' came another sound, followed by a woman's voice screaming.

"Shit, they know I'm here! Please, they're coming for me, please hide me," Alan whispered loudly and as fast as he could. The man and woman stayed motionless on the bed and stared at him with pale faces and shocked expressions, saying nothing. "Is there another way out?" Alan said in desperation.

'Crack!' came a loud noise, as if the door on the next room had been kicked in. Still, the man and woman said nothing. Alan hurried over to the bed, knelt on it and drew open the curtains of a window whose bottom was about a foot and a half higher than the top of the bed. The man and woman huddled together in the far corner of the bed in response.

"Close the window behind me and tell them you don't know anything, then call the police when they're gone," Alan told them. The couple remained silent. It was unclear to Alan if they had taken in any of what he had said.

Alan opened the window. He turned around and climbed out of it backward, slowly lowering himself until he hung by his hands from the outer window ledge, his feet about five feet from the ground below. Then he let go. He landed heavily and fell to the ground in a heap. He stood up slowly, but there was something wrong with his ankle and he was in immense pain. He looked to see where he was and found himself in another long narrow alley; again, one side seemed to end abruptly at a wall. The buildings opposite appeared to be warehouses. In the dim alley lights, Alan spotted a yellow and black metal shutter that was slightly open, about two feet off the ground. He limped to it, laid on the ground and pulled himself under the shutter, then slowly stood up inside and leaned against the wall.

It was almost completely black inside, with the exception of some light coming in from large clear panels in the roofing. Alan could hardly see a thing. He stood there for a minute or two, listening while his eyes slowly adjusted to the darkness. He could now make out a few large piles of wooden pallets all stacked up; the rest was abstract shapes to him. Alan then heard distant sounds. He quickly limped over to the pallets and knelt down behind them—he wasn't going to take any chances. He heard a distant shutter open, followed by several pairs of footsteps and the sound of the shutter closing again. Alan was breathing heavily and his heart was pounding. *What do they want from me?* was the only thing going through his mind.

"So, gentlemen," a stern male voice said from the other end of the warehouse, "do you have the shipment?" Through the gaps in the pallets, Alan saw a dim light switch on at the far end of the warehouse. Four figures stood under the weak light. Something about the way they were standing stopped Alan from calling out to them for help.

"Yes, Mr. Pichaeli. It is outside in the van," replied a timid voice.

"And your friend, who is he? I hope I can trust him for your sake, Costas."

"This is Brian, Mr. Pichaeli," Costas said and indicated the man standing to his left. "He is a good man. He is okay. I have worked with him before, you can trust him."

"He had better be okay. Alright then, let me see the goods," Mr. Pichaeli said. Two figures moved back to the shutter; one was the man pointed out as Brian and the other was a long-haired figure that had been standing next to Mr. Pichaeli. The long-haired figure lifted open the shutter and the two of them exited the warehouse. Mr. Pichaeli and Costas stood silently and waited for their return. After a short while, the two figures returned with the long-haired one holding something small in one hand.

"Here you are," the long-haired figure said in a female voice, handing the item to Mr. Pichaeli. The silently watching Alan was surprised. He had assumed the figure was a man with long hair. Mr. Pichaeli appeared to fiddle with the item for a while.

"Okay, it all seems like good stuff. We will..." Mr. Pichaeli began to say but he was interrupted by the sound of the shutter which Alan had crawled in through opening. "It's a setup!" Mr. Pichaeli shouted. "Kill them both!" A gun appeared in each hand of the long-haired woman as if from nowhere. Shots rang out and it sounded like they were ricocheting all over the building. Alan covered his head with his hands. *I'm going to die,* Alan began to repeat to himself in his mind. He was beginning to lose composure again.

"He has gun!" Alan heard a German-accented man

shout, followed by the sound of people running, then silence. Alan got up and ran as fast as he could to the open shutter at the far side of the warehouse, despite the shooting pain in his ankle. By the shutter, he saw two men lying on the floor, dead. They were the ones he had heard being identified as Costas and Brian. He looked at them for a second, then looked out of the warehouse through the open shutter and saw two black Mercedes cars and a red van speed away.

Alan looked back through the warehouse to see if anyone was coming in through the shutter he had originally come in through, but he could not see anyone. He ran out of the warehouse and onto a road that led away from it. It seemed to head out of the small town, past old abandoned buildings and towards an expanse of fields in the darkness.

After ten minutes of walking, the buildings disappeared altogether and Alan was left on a country road with fields on either side of him. There was nothing but dots of light far off on the horizon and the moonlight to guide his way. After another five minutes or so Alan heard a distant sound. At first, he was not sure what it was but then he saw a pair of car headlamps coming up over the horizon. Alan stood in the middle of the road and waved his arms frantically. The car approached, slowed down, then stopped in front of Alan, its lights forcing him to look away. He walked to the side of the road and the car's lights dimmed as its driver turned off the main beam. The driver's door opened and someone stepped out.

"Please. Please. I need help. Can you help me please, you won't believe what has happened to me tonight," Alan said in a desperate voice.

"What are you doing out here in the middle of the night?" said the driver, a tall woman in a trench coat, standing by her open car door. She was slender and appeared to be in her late 20s. Her hair was dark in color and straight. It sat just above her shoulders.

"I'm lost, I don't know where I am. I've been attacked. Please, can you call the police on your cellphone?" Alan replied.

"Is anyone else with you?" the woman asked.

"No, I just told you I'm lost. I was attacked! Please just call the police," Alan said, his voice becoming a little angrier and more desperate.

"Fucking men! Shut up and put these on!" the woman replied. She pulled out a pair of handcuffs and a gun from her trench coat pockets, throwing the handcuffs so that they landed by Alan's feet. "You men are all the same, think you can just bark your orders and shout out your demands and us women have to do whatever you say!" Alan began to cry and collapsed to his knees.

"No... No, it's not true, this can't be real, not you too. I haven't done anything! Why are you doing this?" Alan thought for a second that maybe none of this was real and that he was having a nightmare. "I haven't hurt anyone," he sobbed heavily.

"Shut up and cuff one hand now!" she said, pointing the gun at him. Alan cuffed one hand. The woman made her way to the front of the car. "Now open the passenger door, pass the handcuffs through the car's interior grab handle and cuff your other hand and then get in." Alan did as he was told, the gun pointing at him all the time. As he opened the passenger door, he let out a gasp. On the back seats was a small Asian man lying completely still on his back. His hands were tied behind his body and he had a clear plastic bag over his head. His eyes were crossed and his face distorted with fear; he was clearly dead, and the last moments of his life had been captured on his face.

"No, please, no," Alan said in a weak voice.

"Get in!" the woman shouted and hit Alan on the back of the head with the butt of her gun. "Rich, powerful men believe they can do whatever they like. I phoned the little Asian fool up and told him that I had accepted his indecent proposal." She said the word 'indecent' with disdain. "The idiot believed me and agreed to meet up. That's when he had an accident with a plastic bag. The foul creature really thought that I would have sex with him to further my career, so here I am taking a drive out to the countryside at 2:00 in the morning to bury him. But it seems as though you'll be doing it for me now, then digging a hole for yourself. Go ahead, say one word and I will shoot you in the head right now. This is his car. Your brains will make a pretty pattern on his car's interior. What's it going to be?"

Alan said nothing, just sobbed quietly to himself. He cuffed his hands together after passing the chain between the car's grab handle and got into the car. The woman kicked the door shut after Alan, then got in the driver's seat and drove off.

Within a few minutes, they passed the old abandoned warehouses and then a minute after that, the derelict car workshop where Alan had been tied to the floor and assaulted by Forsinia, Yohan and Hans. The car drove on and the woman pushed a CD into the car's music player and began to sing along to the song that started to play.

"Oh what a night..." she sang, and Alan's sobbing intensified.

After the song had ended the woman ejected the CD and slowed the car down to a stop. She got out, taking the car keys, and opened the trunk. Alan could not see what she was doing and was sure she was going to retrieve something from the trunk to torture or kill him with, as it was obvious to him that she was completely insane. The idea of death sobered him up a little. He heard the trunk close and saw the woman return to his side of the car carrying a large shovel, which she dropped by the passenger door. She then opened the door.

"Get out slowly and get on your knees," she demanded. Alan did as she said very slowly. She took out a key from one pocket and the gun from the other pocket, put the gun up against his head and un-cuffed his left hand. Alan thought about trying to make a move and going for the gun, but he wasn't sure if he would be able to overpower her, even if she didn't have a gun, because of the condition he was in. Instead, he pulled his hands free of the car's grab handle. "Now cuff them together," the woman continued, and he cuffed his hands back together. She slowly backed up, keeping the gun pointed at Alan's head all the time. "Slowly stand up, take the shovel, then go off over there," she said, motioning with her gun, "and start to dig." Alan got up, took the shovel, and slowly went over to where she had indicated and began to dig.

After half an hour or so, he had dug a rectangular hole about a foot and a half deep.

"Okay, that's enough," came the woman's voice from behind Alan. "Now get Mr. Patel and…" She stopped short. Off on the horizon, two white dots appeared and began to grow larger. A quiet whooshing sound could also be heard. It was a car heading down the road towards them.

"Go and hide! Now! If you run off, I will come after you and shoot you in the back. Now hide," the woman told Alan in a loud whisper. Alan let go of the shovel and walked into the field quickly, going 70 feet or so from the roadside. He crouched down behind some bushes and watched the woman from where he was. As the car neared, Alan saw it was a police car. He wanted to shout out but didn't. *They must be here for her*, he thought, *they'll have guns. I might get out of this alive.*

The woman stood in front of her car with the dead Mr. Patel still on the back seats. Alan crawled further and further away from the roadside and then turned to watch from behind a large wild thorny bush. The police car neared the woman's and stopped 30 feet or so away from hers. Two policemen stepped out with flashlights and began walking towards her. When they were about 15 feet away, she pulled out the gun from her black trench coat pocket and shot them both with one swift move. They fell, dead before they hit the ground. Alan stayed where he was, feeling horrified. He could not believe what he had just witnessed.

"Okay, come back," the woman shouted in Alan's general direction. Alan kept very still. He knew that if she had shot two policemen without a second's thought, then she would be sure to kill him at some point during the night.

"Stand up and come here, I am warning you don't make me mad," she continued in a strained voice, as if talking to a dog that was misbehaving. "COME OUT!" she yelled and started shooting wildly into the field. Alan felt as if the bullets were whizzing past his head.

"AHHHHH!" the woman screamed, then fiddled with her gun for a second. "I will find you someday, somehow! You mark my words, I will," she said, and with that, shot three of the tires on the police car. She went over to it, reached in as if taking something, and then shot something inside. Then she returned to her own car, opened the back door, and dragged Mr. Patel's body out onto the ground and around to the back of the car. Alan watched in silence without moving a muscle. She kicked the passenger door shut and got in the driver's seat. She then reversed over Mr. Patel's body, stopped, drove over his body again, and then purposefully drove over the bodies of the two policemen before continuing on down the road at some speed.

Alan kept still for a while, looking at the silent and motionless police car with its lights still on. He did not want to go back to the road. He did not want to see the bodies, and maybe it was a trap, he thought to himself. Maybe she was also watching the police car from a distance. Alan turned and crawled away from the road, further into the field, on his hands and knees for a good ten minutes before standing up. He continued to walk, almost blind in the blackness of the night. His ankle was still hurting and pain shot up his leg with every step, his right hand and wrist were throbbing and his entire body ached. It was now bitterly cold and Alan's dirty and torn clothes offered him very little protection from the cold weather.

He was beginning to tire fast now and on entering a field of sleeping cows, he collapsed, first to his knees and then flat on the grass. He lay there shivering, and curled himself into as small a ball as he could make. Suddenly out of nowhere, he saw a bright light shining down from above. There was no sound, just intense light. He felt as if he was being lifted and that he was floating. His body felt warm and comfortable. All he could see now was whiteness.

Slowly the whiteness died away and Alan found himself in a small circular room. He was lying on his back, face-up, on a metallic dentist-like chair that appeared to be molded to the ground. He slowly sat up and then realized that he was completely naked, and that both the handcuffs the woman had forced him to wear, and his watch were gone. Although the chair looked like it was made of metal, it was soft to the touch, like polished chrome leather. The room was very warm. He turned and looked around the room, then stopped. There was another metallic dentist-like chair in the room, also appearing to be molded to the floor, only this one was much larger. On it was a cow, lying almost on its back, with its legs sticking up into the air. The cow's stomach was cut open and some of its insides were pulled out and hanging over its sides. Alan instantly felt sick. Then he heard something.

He turned to see a portion of the circular wall melt away. Two suited and helmeted figures stepped through the now-missing part of the wall into the room, and the missing portion of the wall re-materialized behind them. Alan was sure he was in a dream and tried to say something, but words would not come out of his mouth; it was as if he had no control over the muscles in his face. Alan felt sheer terror, he could not move. The figures approached him and as they did so a small portion of the floor rose up, as if it was a candle melting in reverse, to form a metallic pillar about waist height. One of the figures tapped at the pillar and patches of light appeared on the ceiling above Alan. He felt his body rise and float in midair. He tried to scream but was completely paralyzed. The only visible part of the two figures was what could be seen through a clear strip in their helmets that revealed their eyes and a small part of their faces. They had elongated eyes, as if they were from the Far East, but their skin was very pale like albino's skin and the color of their eyes was a bright bluish-grey. Then one of them said something to the other.

"Wootender, wootender, darl, darl," came the figure's muffled voice, which sounded like a male human. Alan did not recognize the language.

"Marsueba," said the other figure. The one that spoke first walked towards Alan as the other one tapped at the pillar once more. Alan's body rotated in the air and positioned itself as if he was on all fours. The figure closest to him reached out toward Alan's buttocks and appeared to stick its entire arm, up to the elbow, into Alan via his anus. Alan felt as though his insides were being jiggled about but he did not feel any pain from this intrusion. He again tried to scream and move, but he was powerless. The figure pulled its arm out.

"Ah shamali duk-duk," the figure said.

"Trepednol," the figure by the pillar responded and then typed frantically at the pillar. Alan's body turned around in the air and floated back down to the chair, landing on it softly. Lights above him on the ceiling flashed wildly, changing color and intensity apparently at random. The pain in his ankle started to subside and a second later it was gone, followed by the pain in his hand and wrist. Next, the pain in his arms, back, and body disappeared. Alan saw the grazes on his arms and wrists vanish as if his body was healing at an immense rate. Then something even more peculiar began to happen. The expanses of fat around his stomach began to disappear as if he was wasting away. Then the same happened to the excess of fat on his chest. His chest tightened and puffed up, as did little muscular ridges in his stomach to form a six-pack. Suddenly he felt the hair on his shoulders, back, chest, legs, and arms begin to retract as if being sucked in by his body. He felt his testicles and penis shrivel and disappear altogether and his limbs and body begin to shrink in overall size but be stretched at the hips. His skin turned slightly paler in color and he felt a rushing and burning sensation on his scalp. Hair was growing out of his head at an immense rate. His pubic hair turned blood red in color and his left chest expanded to form a lump that had the consistency of hard jelly, followed shortly after by his right chest. While this was happening, Alan was screaming as loud as he could, but these screams were only in his head. Then everything faded to black.

Alan slowly opened his eyes. He felt very relaxed and let out a yawn as if he had just woken from a nice long sleep, but within seconds he felt cold and began to shiver. He slowly sat up and found himself in what appeared to be a garden. It was night but he could make out flower beds. He was sitting at the side of a house, on grass that led to its front lawn.

Hesitantly, Alan stood up. Something was not right. Where was he? he thought. It then dawned on him that he was naked. He looked down at himself to see a pair of breasts sticking out of his chest! Then it all came back to him, the figures in suits and the flashing lights, and he began to cry. He looked at his body, as much as he could see through his own eyes, and started to feel himself. His arms were thin and slender, with small, perfectly formed hands that had long fingers and long neat nails at the ends of them. He had a thin waist and broad hips. He had fine straight hair on his head that was about shoulder length, and well-parted circular firm breasts. He reached between his legs but did not feel the normal presence of his testicles and penis. Instead, there was a soft mound that parted in the middle. Alan began sobbing.

After a minute or so he stopped crying and composed himself a little, then put his arms around himself, so as to keep himself warm. He opened the garden gate and walked onto the sidewalk in front. He was in a street full of houses that you would find in any city or large town, and he certainly was no longer in the countryside.

There wasn't a soul in the street and it was extremely quiet as the street lamps shone down their lights. Alan walked along the sidewalk, his head jumbled with mixed thoughts as to what to do next, when he spotted, off in the distance, two figures walking towards him. He ran towards them awkwardly, his bare feet hindering him slightly. The two figures looked up and stopped walking on seeing him approach. Alan stopped a little distance in front of them.

"Please help me, please, I…" Alan started to say but stopped. It was not his voice coming out of him. It was a woman's.

"Wow!" replied the first figure, a scruffily dressed young man who was holding a bottle of beer and staggering a little.

"Oh my god," said the second figure, also a young male holding a bottle of beer. "Hey baby, thought you'd come out for a night's stroll, get a bit of fresh air, maybe bump into some nice fellows like us?"

"Damn you are hot!" added the first man. Then the men looked at each other. Alan instantly read the looks on their faces, turned and ran.

"Hey!" they shouted after him and gave chase. Alan felt himself run easily, and if it were not for the fact that he had no shoes on, he would have outrun them without effort. He leaped over a garden fence and ran around the garden to the back of a house. There was a door on the back of the house and he tried the handle, but it was locked. Alan then saw the two men also appear around the corner of the house, and he turned and clambered over a wooden fence that separated this house's garden from its neighbors.

He landed firmly in the garden of the next house and headed for its back door. It opened, and Alan ran inside. He was in a dark kitchen. He looked around desperately and saw a knife rack, so he went to it and grabbed the largest knife out from the top slot. He held it with both hands in front of his stomach, facing its sharp end away from himself, and turned to face the back door.

Suddenly, the kitchen light came on. Alan turned around. Standing in the doorway, opposite the back door, was a boy, maybe eight years old, wearing pajamas that had yellow and blue teddy bears on them. The boy began to scream and a large wet patch appeared at the front of his pajamas. Within a matter of seconds, a puddle formed by his feet.

"Don't be scared, I won't hurt you, I'm being chased. I just need help," Alan said and put the knife down on the kitchen counter, but the boy carried on screaming. Suddenly a large woman rushed into the kitchen from behind the boy, holding a baseball bat, and hit Alan square on the head.

Alan opened his eyes to find himself in a hospital bed, surrounded by four men, two of whom were standing and the other two sitting.

"We'd like to ask you some questions, Miss," said one of the sitting men. "I'm Detective Sergeant Coleman. May I ask you a few questions?"

"Where am I?" asked Alan.

"It's okay. You are quite safe. You've had a bang to the head, but you're okay now," said one of the standing men, who was wearing a long, white, lab-type coat.

"What's your name?" Sergeant Coleman asked.

"Alan," Alan replied. The four men gave each other puzzled looks.

"Do you remember going naked into someone's kitchen?" Sergeant Coleman continued. Alan's eyes lit up with recollection.

"Yes, yes, two men were chasing me and I ran into a garden and into someone's kitchen. I took a knife to defend myself and a little boy began to scream," Alan said in a heightened voice. The men looked at each other again.

"What is your full name?" asked one of the men who hadn't spoken before.

"My name is Alan Crocker. You don't understand," said

Alan.

"Sir, that's the name of that man that's been in the local news," the man sitting next to Sergeant Coleman whispered into the Sergeant's ear. "The one that disappeared about two weeks ago. They had his wife on the TV crying and asking for information. I think I remember the news report saying the last anyone saw of him was his friends. They saw him leaving a strip club with a woman and no-one has seen him since."

"I went out for a few drinks with some work colleagues and this crazy woman, Forsinia she said her name was, she tricked me! Oh god, and then Batman and Robin were there. I got away but then these men in a gay bar, they tried to kill me. I got away again but the people in the hotel wouldn't help me. I ran and saw these two men get shot and killed, then another crazy woman got me! I thought she was going to help, she stopped her car for me, but she had killed someone, then she killed two policemen! Oh my god. Then men in silver suits; I don't know what they did to me. Please, you have to understand," Alan said all at once through his tears.

The four men again exchanged puzzled looks. There followed an awkward silence, before one of the standing men finally spoke.

"My name is Dr. Wrigley; can you tell me how your pubic hair got that color?" he said.

"The men in the suits did this to my body, all of it," Alan replied.

"Okay, gentlemen, I think that is enough, we will let the young lady get some rest now," the other standing man said.

"No, you don't understand," Alan said.

"You just get some rest, and when we come back, you can explain it all to us, okay?" said the white-coated man. The two sitting men then stood up and they all left the room.

Alan did feel exhausted, and he closed his eyes. His head was sore. He would try to explain it to them again later.

Outside Alan's hospital room the four men spoke.

"We will look into the disappearance of this Alan Crocker and see if she is connected to it," Sergeant Coleman said.

"She is obviously suffering from paranoid delusions. I will check with all the local psychiatric care units to see if they are missing anyone fitting her description. We'll get a psychiatrist up to assess her later. Then we'll move her to a secure unit where she can be held until we find out who she really is," said Dr. Wrigley.

6 LIFE'S A BITCH AND THEN YOU DIE

What a disaster of a day, Claire thought as she walked in through her front door, carrying the letters she had taken from her mailbox outside. She walked into the living room and looked at the pile of mail in her hand. The top letter was addressed to Josh Cooper. Claire threw the pile onto the coffee table without looking through them and the top two letters slid off the table and onto the floor. She dumped her handbag down beside them and slumped onto the sofa, letting out a loud sigh. Then she took her cellphone out of her handbag and checked the time. 11:31 p.m. It was late.

With an effort, she peeled herself off the sofa and walked into the open-plan kitchen. There were two tiny message envelopes on her cellphone's screen, informing her she had new text messages. She knew they would be from her mother, even without opening them to check. She placed the phone on the wooden countertop in the kitchen. The number of samples they had looked through before deciding this was the perfect countertop for their kitchen; that seemed like a lifetime ago.

Claire decided her mother could wait five minutes for a reply, she wanted desperately to get out of her work clothes.

The smell of last night's takeaway 'Meat Feast' dinner still lingered in the air. The smell was so tantalizing yesterday but not so much today, Claire thought as she crossed the kitchen and opened the window above the sink. She picked up the empty pizza box and shoved it down inside the bin. Once upon a time a medium Meat Feast would have meant a cozy night in for two, with a bottle of wine and a cheesy horror movie. The best kind of date night, in Claire's opinion. Not anymore though. Just a medium pizza for one, a Jack Daniels whiskey and Coke, the Jack Daniels portion of the drink probably a little on the excessive side, and a tub of ice cream to top it off. That was the state of Claire's life now.

As Claire ascended the stairs, she began to try to process the events of the day. It started to go downhill from the moment she arrived at work. Her manager, Rachael, had scheduled a one-to-one catch-up meeting for 8:30 a.m. that morning. *Who schedules a meeting at 8:30 a.m. for God's sake?* was Claire's thought when reluctantly accepting the calendar invite. *Your bitch of a manager that's who,* the internal little voice replied. *The first sign of madness is to talk to yourself, isn't it?* was her next thought.

Claire sat facing Rachael in the tiny, windowless HR meeting room. The discussion, if you could call it a discussion since that word implies a two-way conversation, was to address Claire's decline in productivity and general lack of motivation at work. Rachael suggested Claire be referred to the Occupational Health Advisor, which might sound supportive and the right thing for a manager to do, unless your manager was Rachael. In which case it was more like a threat: 'Sort yourself out and concentrate on work, or else.' That kind of underlying threat.

Claire had told Rachael two months previously that she was going through a rough break-up, which would most likely result in divorce. Two months on from that discussion and Claire would now say her marriage was well and truly dead. What did Rachael expect? That Claire should be in top form through these life-altering changes? As if she needed justification for being tearful and distracted at work when her life was crashing down around her.

Claire switched on the bedside lamp on her nightstand. Remembering Rachael's insincere, heavily made-up face made her blood boil. She kicked off her work shoes and one hit the wardrobe door with a loud thud. Then she undressed out of her work clothes, throwing them into the already overflowing laundry hamper, and put on her favorite NYC sweatshirt and tracksuit bottoms.

If she got into bed now, sleep would not come easily; she was too wound up. A hot bath would help her to relax. Claire was tired after her traumatic day, but the thought of soapy bubbles was too appealing to dismiss. Grabbing a clean bath towel from the wardrobe, she walked into the bathroom, put the bath plug into the bath, and ran the water. She poured a large amount of bath foam into the hot water, watching the bubbles appear as she thought of the other events that had shaped her horrendous day.

Josh, or 'That Cheating Bastard' as she now preferred to call him, had phoned her that afternoon to ask if they could meet up that evening after she finished work. She had purposefully worked late in the hope that it would put him off. However, it did not deter him, and he'd even offered to collect Claire from outside her place of work as though he was doing her a favor.

The bubbles were filling the bathtub, little white stress catchers. All Claire had wanted to do after work was to go home, have some comfort food, and watch a mind-numbing reality TV show. Instead, she sat in her soon-to-be ex-husband's white Mustang telling herself she could talk to him without losing her temper. Was it Sarah who had once told her all men who drive white Mustangs are pricks? Or maybe it was Ellen. Not that it was important, the fact was they had been correct.

Claire lit the three tealight candles sitting on the bathroom windowsill and then checked the temperature of the bath, running her hand around and around the inviting hot water. The civility had lasted all of 15 minutes. That Cheating Bastard wanted to discuss arrangements for putting the house up for sale. Claire was not going to make it easy for him to walk away after nine years together. She knew she was being difficult, and felt she had a right to be.

The water temperature in the bathtub was just right, but chocolate to eat while enjoying a well-deserved hot soak would be even more satisfying, so Claire headed downstairs to the kitchen to get some. She took a bottle of water from a kitchen cupboard along with one of her favorite chocolate bars. The notification LED on her cellphone winked impatiently at her. Claire picked up the phone and walked around the counter to draw the curtains over the patio doors.

Please don't let one of the messages be from Josh, she thought. None of the messages were. A pang of disappointment and anger flashed through her, but she dismissed it instantly. Three messages all from her mother, and all asking if she got home safely. Claire typed, 'Yes, I'm home. Very tired. Goodnight mom x', and pressed send. She took a sip of water from the bottle, switched the lights off, and headed back upstairs.

That Cheating Bastard had the nerve to pressure her for a date and time when the estate agent could come to the house to take photos. Claire told him she was busy every weekend for the next few weeks and she was working late most evenings, so that ruled out after work during the week too for the next month. He became frustrated and said, "Be reasonable Claire." An argument followed. It started with Claire shouting,

"Why the hell should I be reasonable? I'm not the one who cheated and wants to throw away everything we spent nine years building together!" The insults came after that and ended with Claire telling Josh to stop the car. He would most likely give her a day or two to calm down and then message her, being all polite. His new girlfriend, 'The Husband Stealing Whore', would persuade him to try again to get Claire to agree to put the house up for sale.

The bubbles looked inviting, rejuvenating and reviving. Claire undressed and dropped her clothes onto the bathroom floor, flicking off the light switch, and gently lowered herself into the bubbly bliss.

Not wanting to go straight home after the argument with Josh, she had made her way to her mother's house in an Uber. Claire had been so angry when getting out of That Cheating Bastard's car, she had nearly ripped the strap off her handbag, trying to get it free from under the car seat where it had caught on something. Slamming the car door had at least annoyed That Cheating Bastard, she could tell by the way he sped off. In truth, Claire's heart felt heavy. When she thought how much she hated him now, compared to six months ago when she was hoping to have his child within the next year.

Ripping off the chocolate bar wrapper, Claire took a large bite and sank lower into the water. It had felt good to have her mother fuss over her and make her soup, adding the croutons for her just as she did when Claire was a little girl. The downside of going to her mother's house, rather than straight home, was that she had to listen to her mother's worried ramblings. Who would Claire meet now that she was 35 years old? Having to sell the house in the current market, they would be lucky to get back what they had invested. How could Claire houseshare at her age? She would surely have to come live with her mother so she could save money. Claire knew that her mother could not help voicing her concerns, but they echoed all the things she had unsuccessfully been trying to put to the back of her mind. She was beginning to wish she had taken a bottle of wine rather than water to sip in the bath. To top it all off, just as Claire had thought she could retreat into her home, she could not find her front door keys in her handbag. They must be sitting on her desk at work. After thinking to herself on the doorstep for some time, debating whether it was better to head back to her mother's and spend the night there or wake up Mr. Johnson who lived next door, Claire had finally decided on the latter.

Mr. Johnson had taken nearly ten minutes to locate her spare set of door keys and then spent another ten minutes lecturing Claire on taking better care of her personal belongings. It was the icing on the 'day from hell' cake. There was no chance Mr. Johnson would be asked to hold her spare set of keys again, that was very clear.

"Ahh," Claire let out a long, deep sigh. The bubble bath was working its magic and she was beginning to relax. Taking another bite of her chocolate bar, Claire closed her eyes and tried to let go of all the tension in her body. She could hear the slow drip, drip from the tap and she tried to imagine her problems dripping away, one at a time, just like the drops.

Suddenly Claire sat up in the bath, listening intently. Did she just hear a noise downstairs? She strained to hear something, anything. A jingle of keys? No, it couldn't be, it wasn't possible—but she had heard something. The kitchen window, it was still open. What if someone had climbed over her garden fence and through the open window? She was alone, naked, and had no means of defending herself. Maybe she was hearing things, just her tired brain playing tricks on her. She looked around for her cellphone. "Shit!" she cursed, whispering. She had left her cellphone downstairs, placing it on the kitchen counter before heading up to the bathroom.

Claire climbed out of the bath as quickly and quietly as possible. She used a bath towel to roughly dry herself and put on her clothes. It took her three attempts before she could tie her long brown hair into a ponytail because her fingers refused to work properly. Still listening intently, she gently opened the bathroom door and stepped out onto the landing.

There! Claire definitely heard a noise, some rustling of paper. Someone was in her house. Her brain raced, maybe the intruder thought she was in bed asleep. It must be after 12:00 midnight by now and all the lights were off. If only she had her cellphone with her, she could call the police and lock herself in the bathroom until they arrived. *Think Claire, think!* she told herself, her heart pounding. The computer in the office! Maybe she could contact the police via some online message.

Claire silently walked into the box room she used as a home office. It was dark, but the blinds had not been closed so the glow from the streetlamps illuminated part of the room. *No, it's too risky,* she thought. The intruder might hear the computer fan spin into life and decide to come upstairs to see what was making the noise. Her brain raced for solutions. Her tablet! No, that was still plugged into the charger downstairs in the living room, it may as well have been on the moon for all the good it did her right now. Maybe she could make it to the front door, it was directly opposite the staircase. What if she met the intruder at the bottom of the stairs? She would need something to defend herself with, but what? Her eyes darted about the room looking for an answer in the dark. She noticed something shining, reflecting in the light from the streetlamps. A silver letter opener sat in the leather pen pot on the desk. *That could work,* she thought. In the dark, it might look more threatening than it actually was, and anyway it was the only weapon available. Claire took the letter opener from the pen pot and tried to steady her shaking hands. It had been a gift from her mother when they had moved into the house. It had a tiny little house engraved into the silver handle, something her mother thought was cute and unique.

Claire walked out of the office and looked over the landing banister to the bottom of the stairs. There weren't any lights on that she could see from her current position. She took an unsteady deep breath and exhaled, then started descending the stairs, avoiding the step she knew always creaked. Her breathing was short and sharp, making Claire feel dizzy. If she could just reach her cellphone, she could call the police once she was out of the house. She stood dead still and held her breath, listening. No sound, nothing.

She decided she would try to get to her cellphone. Carefully she walked towards the doorway that led to her combined living room and kitchen area. The back of her sweatshirt was soaked through from her wet hair, but in the tension, Claire hadn't noticed. Still no sound. Now she felt stupid. Maybe the long, tiring day really had resulted in her losing her mind.

She took a slow deep breath in, then let it out, and her muscles began to relax, loosening her death grip on the letter opener. Then a noise, the shuffling of paper! Claire's body stiffened again. She tried to peer through the doorway, past the half-open door into the combined kitchen and living room area. It was too dark to see anything from where she stood in the hallway. It sounded as though the intruder was in the living room. Claire could make out her cellphone on the kitchen counter, its little notification light winking at her, as though signaling for her to get to it. The counter was only a couple of steps beyond the door. She took a silent step in the doorway. The sound of her heart beating filled her head, making it difficult to focus on any other sounds.

Once in the doorway, Claire's eyes scanned the room. It was dark, and she could only see part of it from the angle she was at. The kitchen and the part of the living room she could see looked exactly as she had left it. Another step into the room towards the counter. Claire held the letter opener tightly, her hand close to her chest. The rustling sound again. She stood still, willing her heart to slow down to its normal pace. One more step and she could grab the phone, turn and run. She held her breath, took a step towards the counter, and picked up the phone with shaking hands.

By now, Claire's eyes had adjusted to the darkness of the room and she could see the kitchen knives sitting in their wooden stand on the opposite counter. Should she try to take one of the knives, in case the intruder chased her out the house and caught up with her? Panic and fear were getting the better of her and she looked from her cellphone to the knives and back again. *Just get out of the house!* the voice in her head screamed.

At the very moment she decided to flee, she heard a noise over her shoulder. Someone was standing right behind her. Claire spun around to find a tall dark figure standing a foot away from her. In her blind panic, Claire screamed and thrust the letter opener towards the dark figure's face. The intruder shouted out in shock and pain, a man's voice. He stumbled backward and fell to the floor.

Claire saw her chance to get out and ran to the front door, her legs feeling as though they had lead weights attached to them. She flung open the door, ran outside and jumped over the two-foot-high wall dividing her property from Mr. Johnson's, then hammered her fists on the elderly neighbor's front door.

"Mr. Johnson, open the door! Please open the door!" Claire kept pounding as she called out to the old man. He could lecture her all day, every day as long as he opened the door right now, she thought. Mr. Johnson's hallway light came on and shone through the front door's stained-glass window. Claire glanced back at her open front door. There was no intruder standing there, but maybe he was just on the threshold. She clicked her cellphone to life with fumbling fingers. Four messages from Josh popped up on the screen, but she swiped them away, dialed 911 and pressed call just as Mr. Johnson opened his front door.

"What the devil..." was all that Mr. Johnson had the chance to say before Claire shoved him back inside his house. As Claire turned to close Mr. Johnson's front door, she heard a voice say her name. She froze, holding the front door very slightly ajar. Someone coughing and then she heard her name again. Claire couldn't understand how it was possible. "What the devil is going on?" asked a puzzled and annoyed Mr. Johnson. Claire held up her hand to silence him. She opened the door slightly, looked out cautiously, and then stepped outside onto the porch steps.

Josh stood on her driveway covered in blood. He was holding one of Claire's patterned tea towels to the left side of his neck with one hand, and what looked like a few crumpled letters in the other.

"Josh?" Claire said in almost a whisper. Josh took an unsteady step towards her and held out the hand that was not pressing the tea towel against his neck.

"You dropped your keys in my..." Josh began to say, but fell to the ground before he could finish the sentence.

"Josh!" Claire shouted and rushed over the wall to Josh's side. She placed her cellphone on the ground and cradled his head in her hands. She was beginning to realize what had happened, her head spinning with the events of the day which had led up to this point.

"Hello? Hello? Are you still there? Do you need assistance?" The tinny voice coming through her cellphone's speaker reached Claire's ringing ears. Claire grabbed the phone.

"Yes! Ambulance! Please! Please send an ambulance!"

7 THE ISLAND

I walked into the room and sat down on the black leather sofa. Dr. Ruben was there, waiting. She swiveled her office chair away from her desk to face me. Her office was quite large, with full bookshelves along one wall and an L-shaped desk in a corner, part of which was under a large tinted window looking out into the facility's courtyard. A big glass coffee table sat in front of the sofa.

"How are you today Jonathan?" she said and gave me a welcoming smile. So far, she had been friendly towards me. She was in her mid-forties with long blonde hair that was tied back into a ponytail. Her looks were slender and attractive, and she seemed to genuinely be a caring person.

"I'm doing okay," I replied.

"Good," she said, and pressed down the record button on a tape recorder that was sitting on her desk. "Let's start. In the last session we talked about your feelings and about your family, but today, I'd like to talk to you about Emily again."

"I don't know what you want me to say. I've already told you everything," I said, trying not to get angry or show any indications that I was annoyed.

"Jonathan, please, I'd like you to tell me again," she said. "Start from the beginning."

"Where should I start, how far back should I go?" I asked.

"Go back as far as you can. Start with what motivated you to go to Amelia Island."

"Okay," I said and sighed. "If I really have to go over all of this again… After graduating college, I started working for J & J Technical Services doing low-level programming stuff, you know, just the boring stuff. It's a good job, I mean it pays okay for what I do, I just don't enjoy it very much, you know?" Dr. Ruben nodded. "The hours are really, really long, like, they give me tasks with deadlines, and there's just no way I can finish them on time if I don't work late. I'm always working past my actual finishing time. Most of the guys on our team work beyond their contracted hours, that is just the nature of the job. The hours are one thing, but the tasks I get given, they're so boring. I don't get to make any of the design choices, I just complete the allocated tasks, check for bugs, that kind of thing. Anyway, it was driving me craz…" I stopped speaking, realizing what I was about to say.

"Go on," Dr. Ruben prompted.

"I didn't mean literally crazy. I just mean that I have a very boring job and my work colleagues are boring. It was a bit of a shock for me after college, you know? At college, I studied hard, but I also had fun, hung out with friends after classes, did stuff on the weekends. After starting work, that all kind of changed and I really didn't like it, but I think that's normal."

"I understand," Dr. Ruben said. "In our first session you said that you like girls, but that you didn't have a girlfriend at college, why do you think that was?"

"I thought you wanted me to tell you about Emily, about how I came to meet her and…" I was saying but Dr. Ruben interrupted me.

"Yes, we'll get to that, but please answer what I ask as

we go along."

"Why didn't I have a girlfriend at college?" I said. "Well, no reason. I don't know, I just didn't meet anyone that, that I liked in that way, that also liked me back, I guess," I said.

"Have you ever had a girlfriend?"

"No. You asked that before, I've told you all of this. What's the point of asking me this all over again?" My voice sounded exasperated and a little angry. *Damn it.* My internal dialog reminded me to keep calm.

"And what about your friends, tell me about them again before we carry on," Dr. Ruben said. Trying not to get upset about the fact that she was asking me the same questions she had before, questions I had already answered, I continued.

"At college, I was friends with, Mark, Robin, Andrew and Alison, and I still have friends from high school too, I guess. Like, occasionally we text and catch up, you know? Organize bowling or something. What has any of this got to do with anything?" I said.

"And Alison is the girl you asked to go to Florida, to Amelia Island, with you on vacation?" Dr. Ruben asked. She already knew the answer.

"Yes," I said, "Alison is the girl I asked to go on vacation with me to Amelia Island."

"Tell me again how that came about, how it was that you came to ask Alison to go with you."

I decided there was no point in protesting about going over everything again. In fact, it would probably make things worse if I did.

"Well, before college ended, Alison and I became quite close, like, good friends. She was in a few of the same classes, we got on well," I explained.

"Did you want to be more than friends with Alison?" Dr. Ruben inquired. "At college, would you have liked to have been more than friends?" I wasn't expecting the question. This was a question she had not asked before.

"In college? No," I said defensively, then backtracked.

"I don't know, maybe."

"I see," Dr. Ruben said in response. "Do you know if Alison had a boyfriend in college, was she involved romantically with anyone?"

"Dr. Ruben," I said calmly, but in protest, "I don't know why you are asking me all of this, how is this relevant?"

"I can assure you, Jonathan, that I am not trying to trick you or anything like that. I am just trying to get a fuller picture of you before you went on vacation," Dr. Ruben said in a reassuring tone.

"She and Andrew had a thing, kind of. She told me that they had hooked up twice and that both occasions were a mistake and they were better suited as just friends. She said that she wouldn't be making the mistake for a third time. It was none of my business, I didn't ask for details."

"Hooked up, meaning they had sex?"

"Yes."

"How did that make you feel?" Dr. Ruben's gaze changed a little when she asked this; she was watching me more intently.

"As I said, it was none of my business."

"You weren't upset that a girl you maybe wanted to be more than friends with had had casual sex with another of your friends?" I didn't like where these questions were going. Dr. Ruben seemed to be much more pressing with them than she had been previously.

"Okay," I said, "yes, I was a little annoyed, but not in some extraordinary way. It happens, you know? I liked her, she liked Andrew, and Andrew was happy to use the fact that she was fond of him to get sex from her. I guess he really didn't like her for more than that. That's how I understood it from the way she explained it anyway. It's no big mystery or secret you've uncovered. It's just life."

"Did you ever talk to Andrew about Alison?"

"No, by the time Alison and I were close friends and she told me about her and Andrew, she explained that it was in the past. Their hookups happened seven or eight months before she even told me. The thought that they hooked up annoyed me a little at the time, it wasn't a big deal to me."

"And after college ended, who did you keep in contact with?" I couldn't understand the relevance of these questions but I knew I hadn't done anything wrong. I would try to be as truthful and honest as I could, and hopefully, I wouldn't have to come back and speak to Dr. Ruben anymore.

"Everyone, mostly online."

"How many times did you meet in person with your friends after you left college and before you went on vacation to Amelia Island?"

"I don't know," I answered, "I'd have to think about it."

"Okay, take your time," Dr. Ruben replied, in a reassuring tone that I was becoming familiar with. I wasn't so sure anymore if she actually cared about me, or was pretending to care about me so that I would say something that she wanted to hear. We sat in silence for about 15 seconds while I tried to recall how many times I had met up with my friends since leaving college. I had graduated in May of the previous year and had started working for J & J Technical Services in late July of that year. I went on vacation on March 23rd of the following year. I tried to average it out in my head.

"I don't know," I finally said, "seven or eight times, maybe, something like that. Once every month or two."

"And which friends were at these meetups and what activities did you do." Dr. Ruben's questions kept on coming.

"It was a mix of people. Sometimes it was with my college friends, sometimes it was with my high school friends. If I organized something, it would be a mix of both groups, that happened twice, I remember those. If someone else arranged something, there might have been their friends there that I didn't know. Just normal stuff. And as for what we did, erm... bowling or the cinema, go out to eat, sometimes we'd go to someone's house and just chill or play video games."

"Did Alison and Andrew attend these meetups? Was there anyone from either your high school or college that always attended or never attended? Did you yourself ever miss any invites to meetups?" I paused for a moment.

"Andrew only came once or twice, everyone else made an effort to be there if one of us had arranged something. Sometimes one or two of us couldn't make it. I think I couldn't make it to a couple of meetups because of working over the weekend to meet deadlines."

"Do you know why Andrew attended less than everyone else?"

"No," I said and gave a shrug.

"On the two occasions when you were the one that had arranged the meetup, did Andrew tell you why he was unable to attend?" I was beginning to get tired of these pointless questions.

"I didn't invite him," I finally said after a pause. "I didn't get on with him particularly well, and he hadn't attended the last few meetups so I just didn't bother to invite him when I arranged something."

"I see," Dr. Ruben said and sat quietly for a moment as if contemplating something. "You said that sometimes you would just 'chill' at someone's house and play video games. During these 'chill' meetups, were any drugs or alcohol consumed?"

"This is bullshit!" I said. Dr. Ruben had finally broken my composure. I stood up and raised my voice. "Why am I here! I didn't do anything! Emily's father attacked me! I just pushed him off of me! I've been here for three days! I told the police everything on the first day and I have already told you all of this too! If they want to charge me for pushing him, then let them charge me! Why do I have to talk to you! What is going on?"

A large man in black pants and a pale blue shirt, who I assumed was a security guard, entered the room and began to approach me. Dr. Ruben raised her hand to indicate to him that she was okay. On seeing her raised hand, he stopped.

"Jonathan, please calm down. I promise you that I am on your side," she said. "As I told you in our first session, a judge has ordered that you are held at this facility and have these sessions with me until an assessment has been made."

"An assessment of what!" I said, still with a raised voice.

"I promise you we will get to that. Now please sit down and try to calm yourself. I know this is frustrating but the longer this takes, the longer we will be here," she said. "Please sit down."

She indicated the sofa with her hand. I looked at her, then looked at the guard, and sat back down. On seeing this the guard stepped back out of the room, but kept a watch through one of the two elongated glass windows in the door.

"Alright Jonathan. Now, were any drugs or alcohol consumed at these meetups?"

"Yes," I said feeling defeated. There was no point in lying, she could find this out from other people. I wasn't sure where Dr. Ruben was going with her questions or why, but if I lied and she then found out, I guessed it could possibly make things worse. "Just beers and weed."

"Alright," Dr. Ruben said, "good. No other types of drugs?"

"No," I said, "just weed."

"Okay, and do you currently smoke marijuana?"

"Yes," I said and looked down at the floor before adding, "sometimes."

"How often," she asked.

"Not often at all," I said, "I might have one joint on a Saturday, you know? Just to relax. If I'm not busy on a Saturday, not going out or doing anything, I might have a smoke. So what? It's legal in some states now anyway." I stopped staring at the floor and looked back up at Dr. Ruben.

"And you live alone?" Dr. Ruben then asked.

"No, I live with my roommate Shawn, we share an apartment."

"Yes, sorry, I remember now," Dr. Ruben said, "You did tell me that previously." Dr. Ruben picked up a notebook from the desk in front of her and flicked through it before stopping at a page. Still looking down at the page, she said, "Once you got the job at J & J Technical Services, you started to look for an apartment so that you could move out of your parents' home. Living alone was too expensive so you searched advertisements online and found someone, Shawn, looking for a roommate. You met Shawn, liked the apartment, thought Shawn was an okay guy and decided to move in." Dr. Ruben stopped speaking and looked back up at me, seemingly waiting for my confirmation of what she had just said.

"Yes, that's correct," I said. Dr. Ruben closed the notebook and put it back down onto the desk.

"And how well do you get on with Shawn?" she asked.

"Fine," I said, "We get on fine. I hardly see him, he's mostly in his bedroom in the evenings or out at the weekends."

"Okay, and why did you want to move out from your parents'?"

"I had a job, I was earning a salary, I thought it would give me more freedom."

"And what have you done with this new-found freedom now that you have it?" I paused and thought about the question for a moment.

"Nothing really," I said. "I can do what I want, when I want, you know what I mean? I smoke the occasional joint and out of the two meetups I arranged, that we spoke about a moment ago, one was at my place. That's all really."

"Okay, let's get back on track. Why did you decide to go on vacation and how did you come to invite Alison to go away with you to Amelia Island?"

"Well, like I was saying, I had been working for about eight months at J & J Technical Services and the workload was just too much and so boring.

"Then, last Friday morning, after I arrived at work, I picked up from where I had left off on the latest project I had been assigned. As I was working, I realized that I wasn't going to make the deadline management had set for me, so I told my supervisor. He told me something like, I had to find a way to finish my part of the project in time. That's when I suddenly lost my temper. I don't know how it happened but I shouted at him. I shouted something like, 'I have been working past my finish time by one to two hours every day since I started here.' As soon as I did it, I realized what I had done. I thought I was going to be fired instantly.

"The supervisor walked away and I started to empty my desk drawer into the bag I take with me to work. My supervisor, David, came back to my desk just as I had almost finished placing all of my personal desk contents into my bag. Alongside him was the department manager, Jennifer.

"Jennifer asked me to go with her to her office. She sounded quite calm when she spoke, so I finished placing my belongings into my bag and followed her to her office. I still fully expected to be fired.

"Once we were in her office, we sat down and she said that David had told her what had happened and that she had quickly checked my key card logs. The employee key cards allow access to certain areas of the building, different areas for different people. Anyway, they also log what time you arrive and leave work.

"To my surprise, she told me that I was right, I had been working well past my official hours and that the company was very pleased with the quality of my work over the past eight months. She said that they didn't want to lose a good worker and that I could take the following week off, paid, and then come back, refreshed, in a week's time. She said in the week that I would be absent, they would check the workload for my project team and make sure it was more evenly balanced amongst the team. I might still have to work late, but it would be much better than it had been once I returned." I stopped speaking and waited for Dr. Ruben to respond. She nodded and said,

"Okay, then what happened."

"I left Jennifer's office and found David. I apologized to him for shouting. He didn't say anything, just gave me a bit of a nod, so I couldn't tell if Jennifer had told him about the week I would be taking off or about her plans for me on my return. Then I just left the office and went home.

"Once I got home, I realized that I actually had the whole of the following week off. I decided I should make the most of it. I thought I might go away, you know? Take a break, have a vacation." I stopped speaking again, expecting Dr. Ruben to ask more of her questions, but she didn't. She just looked at me, listening, waiting for me to carry on, so I did. "I didn't really want to spend a lot of money, I was still paying back the loan I had taken out to buy my car, and paying rent, and trying to save, so I called my uncle who lives in Florida; Amelia Island. We used to visit him when I was a kid and stay, it would be like a cheap vacation for us."

"Who do you mean by 'us'?" Dr. Ruben cut in to ask.

"My parents and I," I said.

"When was the last time you stayed with your uncle on Amelia Island, before this most recent visit?" I thought about it, trying to recall.

"I was nineteen the last time we went, so, almost five years ago. It was in August 2009. We would go every year, or maybe every other year, when I was a kid."

"And what did your uncle say when you asked him if you could visit and stay on this most recent occasion?"

"He was a little surprised, but he told me he would be very happy to have me visit and stay a week. He said that he would try and take a few days off work himself so that we could spend some time together, but that he couldn't promise anything without checking with his work first. After he said that, it made me think about bringing a friend, you know? If he was unable to take time off work, I would still have someone to do stuff with. So, I called Alison. I knew she wasn't working. We'd been texting quite regularly after graduating and in one of her recent texts, she had mentioned that she was still looking for a job. I explained that I had the following week off work and was planning to take a vacation in Florida, Amelia Island, and asked her if she wanted to come along."

Dr. Ruben nodded and gave me a thoughtful smile. She picked up the notebook from the desk again, flicked to a page, read something and put it back down again.

"Okay, and why did you invite Alison and not another one of your friends?" she asked. I paused for a moment.

"I liked Alison, she was nice, we got on well," I said.

"Is that it?" Dr. Ruben asked. "There was nothing more to it than that?"

"Okay," I said, "okay, I hoped that if she came along with me to Florida, maybe something would happen between us, a spark or something. And if it didn't, that would be okay too. Hopefully, we'd still have fun as friends."

Dr. Ruben put a closed hand to her mouth and tapped it against her lips for a few seconds with a look of contemplation on her face.

"Alright," she said, "and how did Alison respond to your offer?"

"She was surprised. At first, she wasn't really sure, but I said we'd have a great time, and that it wouldn't cost her anything, and that I could take her out on my uncle's boat. After a few minutes of me trying to persuade her, she finally said yes. So, I told her I would pick her up at 7:00 a.m. on Sunday morning and that we'd be there by 5:00 or 6:00 p.m. I had allowed for two one-hour breaks along the way. Anyway, as far as I was concerned, she had accepted."

"So, what happened? Why didn't Alison go with you to Amelia Island? You ended up going there alone?" I looked down at the floor and shrugged.

"I don't know," I said. I was silent for a moment before I looked back up and carried on explaining. "I spent the rest of Friday and Saturday before the trip getting ready, you know? Buying stuff I might need and packing. I bought a portable cellphone charger and some new clothes.

"I woke up early on Sunday morning and sent a message to Alison to say that I was on my way to pick her up, but she didn't reply. When I arrived at her house…" I paused for a moment and looked down at the floor again before I carried on. "When I rang her doorbell, Andrew answered." I stopped speaking and stared at the floor.

"Yes, go on," Dr. Ruben prompted me.

"I guess it turns out that Alison and Andrew were having an on- and off-again relationship for a lot longer than she had been letting on. Andrew gave me this look, as if he pitied me, right there at Alison's front door and said something like, 'Sorry bro, she's not going with you, we're back together', or something like that, and closed the door."

I looked back up at Dr. Ruben. "It's not surprising now that I think about it. I had always sensed an underlying tension between her and Andrew back in college. It's just that she never mentioned anything about him in all of our exchanged phone messages. I guess that when I asked her to go with me to Florida on Friday morning, they weren't together, and by the time I went to pick Alison up on Sunday morning, they were together again. That's what I'm guessing, I don't know, how would I know? You would need to ask Alison and Andrew." Dr. Ruben nodded again.

"How did you feel? You had just arrived at Alison's house to pick her up and take her away with you on vacation. You liked her. You were hoping that during this vacation, 'a spark' might happen between you, and now, without warning, you found out that she was with Andrew, who you said didn't really like her but was using her for sex. How did you feel at that moment?" Dr. Ruben asked, and focused her gaze on me.

"I was…" I began to say, then paused to think before

continuing. "At first, I was confused. I stood there outside Alison's front door, stunned, for… it's funny, but I don't know how long for. Maybe it was only a few seconds, maybe it was a couple of minutes. Then I felt a sense of anger and betrayal. I got back into my car and thought about what I should do next." My voice became a little emotional as I said this, but I did my best to control it and I wasn't sure if Dr. Ruben had noticed.

"What you should do next?" Dr. Ruben asked.

"Yes," I said. "If I should cancel the trip and head back home or if I should carry on and drive to my uncle's place in Amelia Island. I decided I wouldn't let what had just happened ruin the vacation, and anyway, if I went back home, I'd have nothing to do and would probably dwell on what had just happened even more."

"Okay," Dr. Ruben said, "let's take a small break." She looked down at her watch. "It's now 10:34 a.m. on Friday the 28th of March 2014. I'm going to stop the tape and we can resume at 11:00 a.m." She was talking into the tape recorder more than to me when she said this. Before she could press the stop button I said,

"Dr. Ruben, can you please tell me what this is all about? Why am I here? Am I under arrest? Did something happen to Emily or her father? Why won't you tell me what's going on?"

"Jonathan, I promise I will explain everything to you. Now would you like me to bring you back something to eat, a sandwich perhaps or a drink?"

"I don't want anything to eat," I said. "They gave me something to eat this morning before they brought me to see you. I would like some water to drink though."

"Okay, very well," she said. "I'll be back soon. Feel free to read any of the magazines on the coffee table," she indicated them with her hand, "but please don't touch anything else." She then pressed the stop button on the tape recorder and left the room. The security guard was still outside of the door, watching me through one of the windows.

I tried to browse through a couple of magazines but I couldn't concentrate. Every time I would read a line my own thoughts would interrupt me. I gave up on trying to read and looked around Dr. Ruben's office.

There were lots of books about psychology on her shelves. I took my time reading the titles on the spines of the books. Not all of them had names on their spines, but most did and a couple of them stood out to me: "The Science of Making Friends" and "The Man Who Mistook His Wife for a Hat". I thought about those two titles for a moment. I had never really thought the making of friends to be a scientific endeavor, but I supposed there was a science behind everything if you dug deep enough. As for the other title, well, the very idea of it being possible scared me.

I turned my head and looked out of the office window into the courtyard. The courtyard was in the shape of a square with grass and trees at its center. It was surrounded by four buildings with pathways that crossed the grass and led to exits at the corners where the four buildings weren't physically connected.

Then I saw, by the building opposite in front of one of the windows, a Northern Cardinal bird trying to conduct a serious battle with its reflection. I watched it as it bobbed and weaved and jabbed at the glass. How could it not realize that it was fighting its own reflection? I wondered.

Watching the bird kept me engaged, and before I knew it Dr. Ruben reentered the room holding a small plastic bottle of water in one hand and a large brown envelope in the other. She handed me the bottled water, placed the brown envelope into a drawer on her desk, and sat down in her office chair. I undid the lid on the water bottle and took a drink from it before placing it onto the coffee table.

"Ready to continue?" she said and clicked the record button on the tape recorder. Why was she recording this anyway? I thought about it for a second and then decided she was probably using the recordings to make the written notes that she kept in the notebook, the one she had read from earlier, because I hadn't seen her actually write anything down on any of the occasions we had met.

"Yes," I said.

"Okay, let's jump forward a little bit. Tell me what happened when you arrived at your uncle's?"

"He asked where my friend was, where Alison was. After I had spoken to Alison, and she had agreed to come along, I called my uncle back, told him an approximate time to expect me on Sunday and asked him if I could bring a friend. He said yes, he had plenty of space, so I guess he was a little confused when I arrived alone."

"What did you tell him?"

"I told him that something came up and that she had to cancel at the last minute. I didn't want to talk about it, you know?"

"I understand," Dr. Ruben said and nodded. "So, let's move on to how you met Emily."

"Oh, well," I said. She was back to pushing me to talk about Emily now. "My uncle told me that he wasn't able to get any time off of work to do stuff with me while I stayed with him." I anticipated what Dr. Ruben may ask me next, how did that make me feel, so I then said, "I felt disappointed, so far the vacation wasn't going very well. I think my uncle sensed my disappointment so he told me I could have the key to his boat while I stayed with him. I guess he was trying to cheer me up. I had taken the Florida Boater Safety Course on the previous visit when I was nineteen. I still carry the Boating Safety Education ID Card in my wallet along with my car license." I looked down at my pant pocket, where I usually kept my wallet, but instantly remembered it had been taken from me by the police before looking back up. "For as long as I can remember, my uncle had always had a boat. I remember, from when I was a kid, that he loved taking it out on the weekends. He keeps the one he has now at Fernandina Harbor Marina."

I paused to see if Dr. Ruben would ask anything but she didn't. "Anyway," I continued, "I didn't really do anything on Monday, I think I was depressed. Alison hadn't come along with me and my uncle couldn't spend time with me during the day. He wanted to take me out so we could do something on Monday night, after he returned home from work, but I said no. I just didn't feel like it.

"I was feeling better by Tuesday morning. I made a couple of sandwiches in the morning and put them into my backpack along with my portable cellphone charger and earphones. I spent most of the day just wandering around, mostly on the beach collecting shells and putting them into my backpack. I also listened to some music on my cellphone, just sitting on the beach and watching the sea. At about 7:00 in the evening, maybe a little later, I decided that I would take my uncle's boat out of the marina and headed over there. I got there just as the sun was setting. As I unfastened the boat's mooring lines, I felt a presence. I looked up and there she was, standing there, watching what I was doing."

"Where had she come from?" Dr. Ruben asked.

"I don't know, I was so busy concentrating on the mooring lines that I wasn't paying too much attention to my surroundings. I was a little bit nervous about taking the boat out of the marina. When I looked up and saw her, for a moment I thought it was someone I knew, or that knew me."

"Okay, then what happened?"

"Well, as I said, I thought she looked familiar, so for a brief moment I just stood there trying to recall who she was, but nothing came to me. I guess she just had one of those faces."

"One of those faces?" Dr. Ruben prompted me to elaborate.

"You know? A face that you think you know, but actually you don't."

"Okay, go on, then what happened."

"She said something like, 'That's a cool boat, is it yours?', and I told her that it was my uncle's boat. Then she asked if I was going out on it alone. I told her yes and explained that I hadn't done this in a while, that I was a little nervous and I was only going to take it out for a short time, into the Amelia River, before bringing it back again. She asked if she could join me."

"Was there anyone else around who saw you two speaking?"

"I didn't notice anyone. My uncle's boat was moored close to the marina's exit," I responded, and as I gave my answer, I felt a shift in my thinking. I no longer thought that I was here because I had pushed Emily's father over. I knew the current situation I was in wasn't normal, but now it suddenly seemed quite obvious. I felt a clarity, a realization that something else was going on.

"Has something happened to Emily? Is she okay? Tell me she's okay," I said, my voice having lost its calm. Dr. Ruben didn't respond to my plea.

"Jonathan," she said, and her voice had also changed a little. It was the sternest I had heard it. "Please carry on." She looked at me with an intensity that made me reconsider any outburst I may have been contemplating to demand answers.

"I was surprised by her request to join me," I said. "I told her she could, without really stopping to think about it, and she stepped onto the boat."

"Describe her to me, what did she look like? What was she wearing?" Dr. Ruben's questions were beginning to scare me a little, but I thought it best to get through them as quickly as possible. I would demand explanations after, even if it meant losing my temper. I ran Emily's appearance through my mind before answering.

"She's white with short brown hair, about jaw length, kind of parted on one side. I think her eyes are green or hazel. She's quite short, maybe five-foot-five and slim. Cute looking. I don't know, I guess her cheekbones are prominent, maybe? She told me she was 19, she looked 19 to 20. Her clothes… well, she had on jean shorts, a striped T-shirt, white and burgundy with the stripes going horizontally across it, and white sneakers."

On hearing my description of Emily, Dr. Ruben's expression changed. It went from being intense, as if she was serious or concentrating, to puzzlement for a brief instant, before becoming blank. I felt as if, in that moment, she was puzzled by something I had said and was trying to conceal that fact from me.

"Give me one moment," she said, then stood up and left the room. Through the elongated windows in her office door, I could see she was talking to the same guard that had been there the whole time. She only spoke to him for a few seconds before reentering the room and sitting back down on her chair. "Sorry about that," she said. "Please continue, Emily got onto your uncle's boat with you." My attention was distracted by the guard outside of the door. He had retrieved a cellphone from a pocket and was speaking into it while staring at me in through one of the office door windows. I tried to ignore him.

"Well, I made sure the boat's navigation lights were on and slowly piloted it out of the marina. We headed southwest along the river. We only went maybe half a nautical mile."

"What did you talk about while you went along the river?"

"Oh, at first we didn't talk. She stood silently next to me in the pilothouse looking out of the windows." I thought that maybe Dr. Ruben hadn't understood what I meant, so I tried to be clearer. "My uncle's boat is a pilothouse boat. It has a full enclosure over the helm, I guess you could call it a cabin." Dr. Ruben didn't ask me anything so I continued. "Anyway, I know that sounds odd, that we didn't speak, but I was doubly nervous. I was piloting a boat in the dark, which I hadn't done before, but the sun had set by then. I was concentrating, and I didn't know what to say to her. I thought she was cute and I didn't want to say anything stupid."

"Alright," Dr. Ruben said, seemingly accepting my explanation, so I continued.

"There's an uninhabited island in the river. It's, I don't know, maybe half a mile across in size. Once we got directly south of it, I told her we should return to the marina, but she didn't respond to that. Instead, she introduced herself and told me her name was Emily and I told her mine."

As I spoke to Dr. Ruben, I would pause after every few sentences. I kept expecting her to interrupt me and ask questions, but now she seemed to once again be paying close attention to what I was saying. I decided to keep talking, without pausing, unless she interrupted me.

"Then Emily pointed out of a window towards the uninhabited island in the river and said something like, 'Do you see that?' I told her I couldn't see what she was pointing at. I remember she looked at me and asked me to take us closer to the island. She tucked the hair on one side of her head, behind her ear and smiled at me." I mimicked the motion with my hand to demonstrate what I meant. "I don't know how to describe it, the nearest thing to say is, when she smiled at me it was like she had the sweetest, most innocent smile I've ever seen. I can't really put it into words, but when she smiled at me like that, I just knew I couldn't refuse her request for me to take us closer to that island."

As I explained the events that had taken place only three days before, it occurred to me that this was the fourth time I was telling this story, of what had happened when I met Emily and how I had come to be on Amelia Island. I had told it at least twice to the police. It was difficult to keep count exactly because I had been asked about some parts more than others and I had told those parts more often. Now, sat in Dr. Ruben's office, telling her again all the things I had told her at least once before, I was giving the most detailed version of events I had given anyone so far. I hoped that by doing this I wouldn't be asked to go over it yet again, and that when I had finished, Dr. Ruben would explain to me what this was all about.

"I piloted the boat towards the uninhabited island just like Emily had asked me to," I said. "I maneuvered slowly while keeping a close eye on the depth display.

"See the thing is, my uncle and his fishing buddy, Russ, had taught me a lot about boating and fishing the last time I had visited in 2009. We had taken my uncle's boat out and gone fishing almost every day for two weeks. I spent more time with my uncle and Russ than with my parents on that vacation. I don't think my parents minded, I think they liked the fact that they were able to spend time alone together.

"Anyway, during that vacation, we had only ever gone out on the boat during the day and my uncle had only let me pilot the boat out of the marina, or bring it back in by myself, maybe twice. But three days ago, with Emily, I was piloting the boat at sundown with no one to watch over me in case I made a mistake. I don't know why I took it out so late instead of during the day, or why my uncle had trusted me so readily with his boat by giving me the key to it. So, I was actually very nervous and took it pretty slow.

"When we were about 150 feet away from the island, I saw what Emily had been pointing to. Tiny flashes of fluorescent yellow light coming from the island, hundreds of them. Emily said something like, 'Isn't it beautiful' and went out from the pilothouse onto the aft deck. I followed her."

"What were the flashes of yellow light?" Dr. Ruben asked.

"Fireflies," I said. "They were fireflies. It looked magical. The way they pulsed and blinked, it was random, yet somehow, synchronized at the same time."

"Okay, then what did you do?"

"Emily thanked me for allowing her onto my uncle's boat. Then she said something like, 'Let's not go back to the marina yet, let's stay and talk awhile. Tell me about yourself,' something to that effect. Again, there was something about the way she looked, the way she asked me, that meant I couldn't say no to her. So, using what my uncle had taught me, I judged that the boat was already facing in an appropriate enough direction, accounting for the river's current and wind, so I didn't need to move it before I lowered and set the anchor. Then we just talked and watched the amazing light show the fireflies were putting on."

"What did you talk about?"

"Well, to be honest, I did most of the talking, just like I am now with you. You occasionally ask me a question and steer the conversation. It was the same with Emily. I told her about where I was from in Virginia, about my parents, about my uncle, how he had always lived alone, he had never been married, just him and his cat, Snowy. I talked about my uncle's boat, about what had happened at work with my outburst and what had happened with Alison and Andrew before I came to visit. I don't remember exactly."

"And what did she tell you about herself?"

"It's funny because she didn't really tell me a lot. She always had another question lined up for me when I had finished speaking. I was kind of flattered. She seemed to be genuinely interested in me as a person. It was nice to talk about myself to someone that wanted to listen. I remember she told me that she didn't have any brothers or sisters, she was an only child, just like me, and that she was nineteen. She was a freshman in college. She lived on Amelia Island, just like my uncle, with her parents."

"Okay," Dr. Ruben said. "Carry on, what did you do next?"

"Well, like I said we talked and the time just seemed to fly by. At some point, I retrieved my cellphone from my pocket to check the time. I had left my watch on the bedside dresser at my uncle's. The time on my cellphone was 10:52 p.m. I remember that because I was surprised by how late it was, and because my phone had been on silent, I had some missed calls and messages from my uncle. The last message said that he was worried because I hadn't been responding, he wanted me to call or message him back and let him know I was okay."

"And did you call or message him back?" Dr. Ruben asked.

"No, I figured I'd message him once the boat was safely back at the marina, but that ended up not happening."

"Alright," Dr. Ruben said and waited for me to continue.

"I told Emily that it was late and that we needed to head back. She just nodded at me and gave me another of her…" I paused for a second, trying to find the right words. "…wonderful smiles. I retrieved the anchor and maneuvered the boat so we were heading in the right direction. Emily stood next to me at the helm, just like she had on the way out of the marina. Again, we didn't speak on the way back, I don't know why. Then, still without saying anything, she took my hand and held it with hers. We just held hands without speaking until we got back to the marina.

"When we were back, I took my time to moor the boat safely, while Emily stayed out of the way on the aft deck. Once the boat was secure, I jumped off onto the floating dock. I extended my arm to offer to help Emily disembark, but she said something like, 'Can't we just stay on the boat a little longer?' Again, I found myself almost instantly saying yes, and I got back onto the boat."

I stopped speaking and thought about what I wanted to say next. I thought that what I was saying might be coming across a little creepy, being that Emily was a little younger than me.

"Go on," Dr. Ruben prompted me to continue.

"I know she is a little younger than me," I said, trying to be tactful with my words. "I admit that, but she's nineteen, and anyway nothing happened between us. She was the one that approached me as I was unmooring my uncle's boat, she took hold of my hand when we were heading back to the marina. I didn't start anything, but yes, I like her, there's something special about her. The way she made me feel that night."

Dr. Ruben diverted her eyes away from me for a brief moment before she spoke.

"It's okay, I understand," she said in a sympathetic tone. "What happened when you got back onto the boat?"

"She said something to the effect of, 'I wish we could listen to music right now,' so I took my cellphone and my earphones out of my backpack. I told her we could listen to music from the playlist on my cellphone, and while I had my phone out, I asked her if I could have her cellphone number. She told me that she didn't have a cellphone anymore. I don't know what she meant by that, and I didn't ask, but she said that she lived at 314 South 5th Street and that I could stop by anytime while I was staying with my uncle."

Dr. Ruben interrupted.

"So, she told you her address and said you could visit?" she asked. Her voice sounded a little skeptical.

"Yes," I said, a little defensively. "I told you that before."

"Alright, carry on, then what?"

"I plugged the earphones into my phone and put one into one of my ears and the other into one of her ears and started to play music from my playlist. She asked if we could go back into the pilothouse because she was feeling a little cold. The temperature had cooled down by then. So we went inside, and I gave her my phone to hold and let her listen to the music while I looked for a couple of blankets, in one of the storage areas under the padded bench seating. I knew that if there were any blankets on the boat, that's where they would be. I had seen my uncle take a blanket from there when he'd had taken a nap and left Russ and me to carry on fishing on one of our fishing trips back in 2009."

I paused again, waiting for Dr. Ruben to ask something, even though I had told myself not to. She didn't say or ask anything, so I continued.

"I found two large blankets. I put one of them over

Emily's shoulders and back, but when I did that, she stood up. She put my phone down onto the padded seat and spread out the blanket, flat on the floor in the gap between the two benches, behind the helm. Without saying anything, she took the blanket I was holding with one hand, and took my hand with her other hand. Then she pulled me down with her onto the blanket she had just laid out." I was replaying the events in my head as I spoke, trying to be as detailed as possible, sometimes using my hands and arms to demonstrate the relevant motions. "She retrieved my phone from the bench, and this time she was the one that put one earphone into each of our ears. Then she lay down, and again she pulled me—not forcefully, but just enough so that I followed her and laid beside her."

"Why do you think Emily did that?" Dr. Ruben asked. "Laid down and made you lie next to her?"

"I don't know. I think she likes me. I think we just connected."

"Okay, go on," Dr. Ruben said, giving a small nod for me to continue.

"We were lying on the blanket, and she turned over so that her back was to me and pulled my arm over her, so that we were kind of cuddling with her back against my chest, listening to the music on my phone. She pulled the other blanket over us, and we just stayed like that listening to music."

"And the whole time this was happening neither of you spoke?" Dr. Ruben asked.

"No," I said.

"And did anything else happen? Did she kiss you? Did you kiss her?"

"No, we just laid there, cuddling and listening to music."

"Didn't you find it odd, what was happening? Doing what you were doing? Without speaking? With a woman five years younger than yourself, who you had only just met?"

For a moment I thought that what Dr. Ruben had just

asked should have made me angry, but it didn't. Explaining to her what had happened in the pilothouse with Emily, us cuddling on the floor and listening to music, had made me relive those moments in my head, which had actually made me feel calm for a moment.

"No," I said, "it didn't feel odd. It felt right, it felt perfect."

"Okay," Dr. Ruben said. "Then what happened?"

"Nothing. I don't know how long we stayed like that on the floor. Time seemed to be... I don't know, it was like time didn't exist, I can't explain it. I don't know how long we laid there like that listening to music. I remember I felt happy and warm, and the playlist I had picked was from my ambient-chill collection. I fell asleep. When I woke up, it was morning, with light shining in through the windows of the pilothouse. My phone was dead and Emily was gone."

"You fell asleep cuddling someone that was effectively a stranger to you? Someone you thought was cute. That's a little unusual, isn't it? Normally in a situation like that, you wouldn't be able to sleep, even if you tried," Dr. Ruben said. I wasn't sure what point she was trying to make.

"I don't know," I said, "maybe. I don't know if that's unusual or not, but it is what happened."

"Okay. You wake up, it's morning, light's shining in through the windows, Emily is gone. What do you do next?"

Before I could answer Dr. Ruben's question, there was a knock on the door that startled me. It was the guard. "Excuse me a moment," Dr. Ruben said, and left the room to talk to the guard just outside of the room. I watched through the glass in the door as he leaned over, said something in her ear and handed her a brown envelope. She said something back to him and then reentered the room, where she sat down and put the envelope into the same drawer with the one from earlier.

"Sorry Jonathan, please continue," she said.

"Well. I got up and looked out of the windows to check if Emily was on board, but she wasn't, so I started to put the blankets away. When I picked up the blanket we had been using as a cover, there was a necklace on the blanket that we had been lying on. It was a necklace with a purple elongated diamond-shaped pendant on it. I assumed, I don't know, that Emily had left it there on purpose, you know? Like, since she didn't have a cellphone. I thought that it was her way of saying, 'I want to see you again,' because she had told me her address and left the necklace so that I could return it to her."

"Okay," Dr. Ruben said. I couldn't tell from her voice whether she believed me or not. "Had you seen it around Emily's neck the previous night?"

"No," I answered, "it must have been under her T-shirt."

"So, when you saw it, how did you know it was hers?"

"It must have been I said, she placed it there for me."

"Alright," Dr. Ruben said. I thought maybe I sensed a hint of doubt in her voice. "What did you do next?"

"I picked it up and put it in my pocket. I put the blankets back neatly into the storage units and got my cellphone and backpack, left the boat and marina, and walked back to my uncle's place, which took about an hour.

"I didn't know what time it was. I hadn't bothered to plug my phone into the portable charger in my backpack, and when I walked into the house, my uncle was in the kitchen eating breakfast. The time on the kitchen clock showed that it had just gone past 7:15 a.m. My uncle was actually pretty cool, which surprised me. He said something like, 'Oh you're alive then? Good. You have a cellphone, next time use it,' and something about not being my mother, and if I hadn't returned by that night he would have had to call the police to report me missing. He offered me breakfast but I said that I wanted to shower first, so I went to do that. As I took off my jeans, the necklace fell out of my pocket onto the floor, and I put it onto the bedside dresser. I plugged my phone in to charge while I showered. After I got out of the shower, I got dressed. I saw the necklace next to my watch on the dresser so I put it on around my neck, over my T-shirt."

"Why did you do that?"

"Well," I said, "I was planning on returning it to Emily. I thought that it would be funny, you know? If I called at her door and she answered and saw it around my neck. I thought I was being clever. Like, she had been clever by giving me a message when she had left it, and I would be giving her a message back by wearing it when I called at her door."

"What message did she give you and what message were you planning on giving back?" Dr. Ruben asked.

"You know, she left the necklace as a message to say, I like you and I want to see you again, and I wore it to her house so when she answered the door and saw me wearing it, I would be saying, I got your message and I like you back."

"I see," Dr. Ruben said. Again, I couldn't tell if she believed what I was telling her. "Carry on," she added.

"So, like I was saying, I got dressed, then went downstairs and had some cereal for breakfast. My uncle had left for work by the time I went back into the kitchen. I decided I would drive to Emily's house in my car. I was hoping that, if I asked her to come out with me and she said yes, then maybe we could drive somewhere."

"Okay," was Dr. Ruben's response. I thought she might ask me where I was planning to take Emily in my car, but she didn't and I continued.

"I drove to Emily's house and pulled into her driveway. Her house was only ten minutes' drive away from my uncle's. When I pressed the doorbell, a man in his mid- to late 40s answered the door. I said, 'Hello, I'm a friend of Emily's, is she home?' or something like that. He didn't answer. He stared at the necklace around my neck and lashed out, trying to grab me. He was shouting, 'you bastard, I'll kill you!' We struggled for a moment in the doorway and I pushed him. He tore my T-shirt because he was holding on to it as he stumbled and fell backward. He landed pretty hard on the floor inside the doorway of his house, and I ran back to my car, got in and locked the doors. He got up and ran to my car. He was trying to open the driver's door, pulling on the handle and banging on the window with his fist and kicking the door, screaming he was going to kill me. I reversed out of the driveway and drove back to my uncle's house. I don't know what he told you, but he attacked me first. That's why I pushed him. I assumed he was Emily's father, and he was angry because he guessed that I was the person that Emily had stayed out all night with." I stopped speaking and waited for Dr. Ruben to say something.

"Alright," she said, "what happened next?"

"What do you mean, what happened next? You know what happened next," I said, exasperated. "I drove back to my uncle's house. I went to the bedroom I was staying in and lay on the bed. I stayed there, staring at the ceiling. I was upset. How was I meant to feel? I had met an amazing girl who seemed to like me, and when I went to see her, her father freaked out on me. So I just lay on the bed for I don't know how long, replaying things in my head: my time with Emily and her father's reaction.

"The next thing I know was that there was a loud sound, a cracking thud. The police smashed open my uncle's front door and came into the house. They found me in the bedroom and dragged me out so roughly that they left bruises on me. They didn't read me my rights or tell me why I was being arrested or anything! How is that even legal?"

I stopped speaking. I wanted Dr. Ruben to say something, give me an explanation, but she didn't say anything. She just looked at me, waiting for me to continue, so I did.

"At the police station they finally told me I was under arrest for assaulting Mr. Hobson, who I assume is Emily's father, which is bullshit by the way, because as I said before, he attacked me. They took the necklace off of me, and my wallet and my phone. They fingerprinted and photographed me. They swabbed me for my DNA and they started to ask me a bunch of questions. My name, my date of birth and address, whose house was I in when they arrested me and why was I there. Where did I get the necklace? A whole bunch of shit like that." I was beginning to get a little angry again. "I answered everything they asked me. I told them everything that I've told you. Then later on that same day, on Wednesday, they brought me here to talk to you, and I told you the same thing I told them, and I'm telling you the same thing again now! I've been kept here for two days because you say a judge has said I have to talk to you? Why?"

"Okay," Dr. Ruben said, and she turned and opened one of the drawers on her desk. She retrieved a brown envelope from it. I assumed it was one of the envelopes I had seen her put into that drawer earlier. She fished around inside of it for a moment before bringing out three photographs, all of young women who appeared to be in their late teens or early twenties. She placed them on the glass coffee table facing me. "Which one is Emily?" Dr. Ruben asked. I looked down at them, puzzled, but responded quickly.

"None of them," I said. "None of them look anything like her." I wanted to say something else, but I didn't know what to say, so I waited for Dr. Ruben to reply.

"Yes," she said, "you're quite right, I'm sorry. That was an unfair trick, but I had to do that." She picked up the photographs from the glass coffee table and put them onto her desk. She then retrieved a second envelope from her desk drawer, took three different photographs out of it and placed those onto the coffee table facing me without saying anything. Again, they were of three young women. I recognized Emily right away.

"That's Emily," I said and pointed at the photograph. "That's her, but she looks a little younger and her hair is different, longer."

"Yes," Dr. Ruben responded, "you are correct, that is Emily." She then removed the second set of photos from the coffee table and placed those onto her desk before turning to face me again. "When the police arrested you, they also removed some of your belongings from the bedroom at your uncle's. Inside your backpack, they found some marijuana wrapped up in a small tin, along with paraphernalia used to smoke it." Dr. Ruben stopped speaking and waited for me to respond. I sensed myself getting angry and tried to contain it with only partial success.

"So what!" I snapped back at her.

"When was the last time you smoked marijuana?" Dr. Ruben asked, calm. She didn't seem to be responding to the raised level of anger in my voice.

"I smoked a joint on the beach, on Tuesday, before I headed over to the marina. I brought a few joints' worth of weed with me on vacation, big deal," I managed to say, but then lost my temper and shouted, "Tell me what is going on!"

"Alright, Jonathan. I want you to prepare yourself for what I am about to tell you." Dr. Ruben paused so that there was a brief moment of silence between us. "Emily Hobson was murdered in August 2009. She was raped and killed, and her body was dumped on the uninhabited island in the Amelia River opposite Fernandina Harbor Marina."

"What! That's not possible!" I said, almost shouting. My heart began to beat faster, and I felt a sensation spread from my stomach as if I was on the drop part of a rollercoaster.

"I'm afraid it's true, Jonathan," she said in a somber tone, and retrieved another envelope from her desk drawer. She removed a photograph from inside of it and placed it onto the coffee table facing me. It was of a plush toy, a white knight holding a shield.

"Have you seen this before?" Dr. Ruben asked. Before I could say anything, she spoke again. "Emily's father, Mr. Joseph Hobson, is an ex-police officer, retired early. Naturally there is a lot of sympathy toward him from the local police department, especially since they weren't able to convict anyone for the murder of his daughter. Unofficially, Mr. Hobson was kept informed about your arrest, including your name. And do you know what he remembered? He remembered that the day before his daughter went missing in August 2009, Saturday the 22nd to be exact, Emily had returned home with this plush toy." Dr. Ruben tapped the image on the coffee table with her forefinger. "She had been out with friends in Jacksonville. When her father asked her where she got it from, she told him that it was her knight in shining armor, Jonathan. That's quite a coincidence, don't you think? She told her father that she had named it after a boy who had won it for her on a claw machine at an arcade in Jacksonville."

I stared at the photograph, but my mind was having trouble focusing on the meaning of what Dr. Ruben was saying, and I couldn't respond.

"Since your arrest on Wednesday, the police have been quite busy," Dr. Ruben continued. "They have spoken to your parents and uncle, of course, and one of the things they discovered was that on the last day of your vacation to Amelia Island, on Saturday the 22nd of August 2009, before heading home to Richmond, Virginia, you, your parents, your uncle, and your uncle's friend Russell Keeler went and did some shopping in Jacksonville, about twenty miles south of Amelia Island. After shopping, the last thing you did before leaving your uncle and Russ to drive home with your parents, was to go to Dave & Buster's arcade, bar, and restaurant. Police have confirmed that you were there with your family at the same time that Emily was there with her friends."

With Dr. Ruben's last sentence in my head, it suddenly clicked into place and I began to cry.

"Yes," I said, sobbing, "yes, I remember. It was the last day of our vacation before we went home. After shopping in Jacksonville, we were hungry and my parents asked where I wanted to eat. I said Dave & Buster's. I thought it would be fun. After we had finished eating, my parents gave me money to get a Power Card, the card you use to play the games with.

"I had been walking around for a while, playing a few games, when I saw a girl in front of a claw machine, alone. Emily. She was trying to win a plush dragon. I stood watching her. She played until she ran out of credit. I don't know why, but I went over to her and said, let me try. She looked and me, smiled and said, 'Okay.' I completely missed the plush dragon with the claw, but it grabbed a plush knight next to it and we laughed. The claw machine was full of green dragons and white knights. I handed the knight to her and said that I was sorry it wasn't a dragon.

"She was surprised and asked if I was really giving it to her. I told her that I was, and she asked me for my name. I said it was Jonathan, and she told me that she would name it after me.

"I was going to ask her what her name was when three girls approached us and asked her what she was doing, they wanted to move on somewhere else. I think they were her friends. She told them she wasn't doing anything, turned to me, kissed me on the cheek and said, 'Thanks for Jonathan, Jonathan,' holding up the toy. Then she said, 'It was nice meeting you. I hope I see you again,' and went off with her friends. I wanted to say something, ask her for her name and phone number, but I didn't. A minute later Russ came over and told me my parents were looking for me and that it was time to leave." I tried to compose myself and stopped crying. "But she can't be dead!" I added harshly. "She's alive, I saw her three days ago."

Dr. Ruben didn't respond to what I said.

"After Emily's disappearance and murder," she said, "the police did follow a line of inquiry, trying to find who the young man was that had won the plush toy and given it to Emily. Unfortunately, the hard drive containing the security footage at the arcade was overwritten every thirty-six hours. There was a technical reason for that, if I remember correctly; it was a multi-hard drive system and one of the hard drives had failed and hadn't yet been replaced.

"The police tried to retrieve the security footage from the arcade, but they were too late. Another reason why you were never found was that, as luck would have it, the nearest public surveillance camera wasn't functioning. Because of that, the police were unable to find which cars had visited the arcade on that day.

"That line of inquiry was also downgraded and less publicized when an older lady came forward and said that she believed she had seen Emily getting into a car with a middle-aged man. However, she couldn't remember any details about the model of car, or even its color, apart from saying it was a light one.

"You see, Jonathan," Dr. Ruben continued, "the reason you were brought to this facility was so that your mental state could be assessed by me. Once you told the police the story about meeting Emily at the marina and taking her on a boat ride, the detectives interviewing you eventually believed that you thought you were telling the truth." Dr. Ruben's voice became more sympathetic as she spoke. "However, the story you told is impossible. Emily Hobson is dead.

"My assessment of you is that, although you are clearly an intelligent and articulate young man, you were in a delusional state on Tuesday when you went to the marina to take your uncle's boat out onto the river. Let's look at the evidence. Before going to Amelia Island, you were under a lot of stress at work, so much so that you lost your temper and shouted at your supervisor, risking losing your job. Lucky for you that you had a sympathetic employer who, instead of firing you, allowed you to take a break from work.

"Then you invited a girl, who you were clearly fond of, to go away with you on vacation, and as far as you knew she had accepted your invitation. However, at the very moment you were expecting to collect her, Andrew answered her door. Andrew, the young man who, according to you, was only using Alison for sex. The mental hurt which something like that can cause is substantial, knowing that she would rather let herself be used by someone like Andrew than go away with you on vacation." Dr. Ruben's last sentence pierced me like a dagger and I jerked back on the sofa with hurt, but she kept on going. "Also, you smoke marijuana. Now, you say you do so only occasionally. It's difficult for me to know how often you smoke it, but the fact that you brought some along with you, from Richmond to Amelia Island, leads me to believe that you smoke it a lot more often than you have admitted to me, and there are plenty of studies that show a link between marijuana use and psychosis.

"You yourself admitted that you had smoked some on the beach, right before you headed to the marina, to your uncle's boat."

I wanted to protest what Dr. Ruben was telling me, but said nothing and looked down at the floor.

"And then we come to Emily herself. An attractive young woman whom you had met almost five years ago in that arcade in Jacksonville; someone you clearly liked, someone that had responded positively to you, who named the toy you won for her after you, and who kissed you on the cheek before you were pulled away from each other by her friends and Russ.

"You see, what I think happened is that when you returned to Florida, to Amelia Island, for the first time since 2009, you were under a heavy mental strain—from your work, and especially from being rejected by Alison. Then your marijuana use put that mental stress over the edge into a delusion.

"Being back in Florida triggered something subconscious in you: memories of the positive encounter with Emily five years ago. Your mind brought her back to make up for you being rejected by Alison. It gave you the perfect romantic evening with her on a boat, on the Amelia River, watching a magical light show put on just for you by fireflies."

As Dr. Ruben spoke, I began to cry silently. A stream of

tears rolled down my cheeks and collected on the floor between my feet.

"But none of it was real, Jonathan. It was all in your mind. You were alone on that boat."

Dr. Ruben stopped speaking and there was silence in the room as I thought about what she had told me. I thought about the book title I had seen earlier, "The Man Who Mistook His Wife for a Hat" and the Northern Cardinal bird I had seen battling with its own reflection on the building opposite. If a man was capable of being unable to tell the difference between his wife and a hat, and if birds couldn't tell they were battling their own reflections, maybe I was capable of hallucinating a perfect evening with Emily aboard my uncle's boat. I looked back up. Dr. Ruben had retrieved a box of tissues from somewhere and was holding it out to me. I took one, wiped my eyes and regained my composure.

"But I don't understand," I said. "If it was all in my head, what about the necklace? Whose necklace did I find on the boat? How did I know Emily's address, and how did the police know to look for me at my uncle's house?"

"Well," Dr. Ruben said, "your last question is the simplest one to answer first. During your altercation with Mr. Hobson, he got a good look at your car and at your license plate. It was fortuitous that Mr. Hobson's car was at a local workshop undergoing servicing, otherwise he would have pursued you, and who knows how that might have ended.

"After you sped away, he called the police. Since he is an ex-police officer who was reporting on someone that was, to his mind, involved in the murder of his daughter, an immediate APB was put out for your vehicle. It wasn't very long before an officer drove past your uncle's house, saw your car in his driveway and called for backup."

Dr. Ruben turned and retrieved yet another envelope from her desk drawer. "You see the gentleman standing outside the door?" she asked, indicating him with her head.

"That's Detective McConnaughey." He wasn't a security guard after all, he was a policeman. "I asked him to do a search for me when I stepped out of the room before, and this is what he found." Dr. Ruben removed a piece of paper from the envelope and put it onto the coffee table facing me. On it, printed in color, was an image of Emily from the waist up. She was smiling and had on a horizontally striped T-shirt, white and burgundy. Her hair was similar to how I remembered it from when I met her at the marina—or maybe more accurately, how I remembered it from my delusion of her at the marina.

"Emily went missing on Sunday the 23rd of August 2009. Her body was found a week later, on Sunday the 30th of August. A fisherman, anchored not far off the uninhabited island in the Amelia River, spotted it from his boat. This photograph, along with several others, was used to appeal for information to help find her via regional news outlets and the internet. It and others were used again when the news outlets reported that her body had been found. You probably saw this image at some point on the news and subconsciously incorporated it into your delusion."

"But what about her address?" I said. "She told me her address.

"That's been looked into," Dr. Ruben replied. "It's unlikely that Emily's address was given out directly on the news, but it looks like a few TV interviews were conducted with her father in front of the family home. If the door number was visible in the news footage and you saw it, you probably subconsciously worked out her address. After all, you have been visiting Amelia Island regularly since you were a child. No doubt you are familiar enough with it to know an address from seeing it on the news."

I thought about what Dr. Ruben was claiming. I wasn't sure I believed her, but I had to concede that she was the expert on this topic, judging from the number of psychology books on her office shelves alone. If she said that it was possible, I had to accept that maybe it was.

"What about the necklace?" I then asked.

"Yes," Dr. Ruben said and paused before continuing. "The necklace. The necklace is Emily's necklace." As soon as she said that I wanted to interrupt and ask how that was possible, but I realized that she would explain it, so I let her continue. "You see," she said, "when you were first arrested, the police naturally thought you may have been responsible for her murder. When Emily went out on Sunday the 23rd of August 2009, the last day she was seen alive, a day after you returned to Richmond, she was wearing that necklace. It was a gift for her 18th birthday from her mother. Apparently, it was part of a set that included earrings and a bracelet, but she only ever wore the necklace according to her mother. She liked the purple sapphire pendant.

"When her body was found, she wasn't wearing the necklace. Detectives hypothesized that maybe the killer had taken it as a trophy, or perhaps had dropped it in the river or taken it to sell. They didn't publicize to the media that the necklace and its unusual pendant were missing, in the hope that the killer might try to sell it. They spoke to a lot of jewelers and pawnbrokers, even staked out a few of the most popular stores, known for criminals trying to sell stolen goods. Eventually, about three months after Emily's body was found, police released the information about the missing necklace to the media and news outlets in the hope that someone from the public might come forward with information about it, but the necklace never appeared.

"There was some internal criticism from within the police department about the delay in going public about the missing necklace. Some believed it would have been better to publicize the fact that the necklace was missing soon after the body was found, because when it was finally made public, the media coverage about the missing necklace, in relation to Emily's murder, was a lot less than when the media was reporting that her body had been found and in the immediate weeks after.

"The police were, however, able to recover what they

believed to be the murderer's DNA from the body due to the sexual assault he had carried out on Emily before killing her and dumping her body. Unfortunately, the DNA didn't match anyone on the national DNA database, so unless the killer's DNA was added to the database for another crime he committed in the future, obtaining his DNA wasn't an immediate breakthrough.

"You, Jonathan, were ruled out as being the murderer yesterday, once the DNA results from the swab that was taken came back. Of course, the police were also able to confirm that you had left Florida the day before Emily went missing.

"Another thing the police knew was that whoever murdered Emily must have had access to a boat, in order to have been able to dump her body on the island in the Amelia River."

As Dr. Ruben said this last sentence, I was filled with a sense of dread and interrupted her.

"No," I said, "it's not possible. You're saying my uncle had something to do with a body being found on the uninhabited island, because I found the necklace on his boat?" I didn't want to say Emily's body because I still wasn't one-hundred percent convinced that Emily was dead. "My uncle would never hurt anybody," I added.

Dr. Ruben paused for a moment before speaking again.

"Actually Jonathan," she said, "a lot of boat owners were investigated at the time, including your uncle. On the morning of Sunday the 23rd, the day Emily went missing, your uncle drove south to Miami. He spent the day there with some friends, and on Monday attended meetings there connected to his job in Jacksonville. He didn't return home until Tuesday afternoon. His whereabouts and the timeline he gave were corroborated. When he was originally questioned and asked if he was willing to provide a DNA sample, as were many men that lived in the area and owned boats, he agreed to provide one. Obviously, his DNA wasn't a match."

"So how did Emily's necklace get onto my uncle's boat? How do you even know it's Emily's necklace?" I cut in to ask.

"Oh, it's Emily's necklace all right," Dr. Ruben said. "Emily's mother wanted to get her something extra special for her 18th birthday. She found a jewelry set comprised of the pendant with its necklace, a bracelet, and earrings online. The website she bought it from was for a store in London, England: a store based in London's Hatton Garden, a street famous as London's jewelry quarter, and the center of England's diamond trade. It was not a mass-produced set of jewelry. The pendant is a valuable item, but it is unlikely that an opportunistic criminal would have killed someone for it.

"The relative uniqueness of the pendant is why Emily's father reacted the way he did when he answered the door and saw it around your neck. He knew it was Emily's pendant, the one she had been wearing when she went missing."

I was puzzled by what Dr. Ruben was saying. If I had hallucinated my boat ride with Emily, and the necklace I had found on my uncle's boat really was Emily's, and if my uncle wasn't involved in her disappearance and murder, then what exactly was she telling me? "Police forensics," she told me, "found a fingerprint on the back of the pendant on Wednesday and were able to match it to someone by Thursday afternoon, yesterday. That person was arrested shortly after." I sat up a little straighter, eager to hear what she would say next.

"In 2012," she said, "a man called the police because he saw another man, one he didn't recognize, acting suspiciously and entering his neighbor's garage. The police arrived in time to find the man in the garage and arrested him. As it turned out, he was trying to retrieve a lawnmower that he claimed he had sold but had not received full payment for.

"As is standard procedure, he was photographed and fingerprinted while being processed at the police station, but his DNA was not taken, since the crime was a misdemeanor stemming from a dispute over a lawnmower. The law allowing police to take DNA samples from anybody under arrest for any crimes, regardless of whether it was relevant to their arrest, was not passed by the Supreme Court until June 3rd, 2013.

"The man who was arrested, fingerprinted and photographed in 2012 was Russell Keeler—Russ, your uncle's fishing companion. The fingerprint found on the back of Emily's pendant matched his right-hand forefinger print, taken from him for the burglary he had committed." Dr. Ruben looked at me as if she was watching for a reaction, but I was too shocked to say anything. "When he was arrested yesterday," she continued, "he of course denied having anything to do with Emily's disappearance, rape and murder. But when he was told that his DNA would be taken and it was only a matter of time before the results came back, proving that he had had sexual intercourse with her before she was murdered, he confessed."

I wasn't quite sure why but, on hearing what Dr. Ruben had just told me, I began to cry again. Maybe it was because I liked Russ, my uncle's fishing buddy. He had always been kind to me and taught me various things about boating and fishing. Maybe it was because I couldn't quite believe any of what was happening.

"I want you to prepare yourself for what I am about to tell you next," Dr. Ruben then said. I felt myself tense up, hearing this. "Russell Keeler told the police that he was watching you with Emily at the arcade that afternoon, on Saturday the 22nd, back in August 2009 in Jacksonville. How, according to him, you had interacted with her and how she had flirted with you.

"After everyone else left the arcade, you with your parents and your uncle, Russell stayed behind and waited. Once Emily left, he followed her all the way back to Amelia Island in order to find out where she lived. Then, because he knew your uncle was leaving Amelia Island early on

Sunday to go to Miami for a couple of days, he drove to your uncle's house that morning at a time he knew your uncle would have already left.

"You see, Russell Keeler was the type of man that found it difficult to hold down a regular job, so he was always moving from one employer to another and he had a lot of free time on his hands. Because he was a close friend of your uncle's and loved boating and fishing, your uncle was generous enough to, on the odd occasion, allow Russ to take the boat out for a spot of fishing alone. In order to facilitate this while he was working, your uncle left a spare key for the boat under a plant pot at the side of his house. If anyone else found the key, they wouldn't know what it was for, so your uncle felt safe in leaving it there, and Russ had only taken the boat out alone on a handful of occasions. He would always phone your uncle to ask for his permission first or arrange it with him in advance.

"That Sunday morning, Russell took the spare boat key from under the plant pot at your uncle's house. He then drove to where Emily lived and waited, not far from her house, for some hours. When she finally left home in the early afternoon, to walk to a store a few blocks away on South 8th Street, he saw her leave and approached her in his car. He told her that he recognized her from the arcade the previous afternoon, and said that he was the uncle of the boy who had won her the plush toy. He told her he was on his way to see you and that, if she wanted, he could take her to you. Apparently, she agreed. The brief encounter you had with Emily at the arcade must have left an impression on her, because she was eager to see you again." On hearing this, I suddenly felt sick. Dr. Ruben must have sensed this, because she stopped speaking. I picked up the bottle from the coffee table and drank a little water in an effort to settle my stomach. Dr. Ruben then resumed explaining the sequence of events to me, as confessed by Russ to the police.

"Emily got into Russell's car, this was what the older

woman that came forward to the police as a witness had seen. He told her that you were waiting for her on a boat. Russell drove Emily to the marina, and there he told her that your uncle's boat was his. When Emily saw that you weren't aboard, Russell told her you were waiting for her on another boat anchored in the Amelia River with your parents. We don't know how, but somehow, he convinced Emily to go along with him on your uncle's boat, out onto the Amelia River.

"The forensic analysts say that, at some point during the boat ride with Emily, Russell must have held her pendant between his thumb and forefinger, perhaps in order to admire it. By holding it, he transferred his fingerprint to its back. Eventually, when Russell tried to seduce Emily on the boat by taking the blankets out of storage and trying to get her to sit on them in the boat's pilothouse, she realized that she had been tricked. Russell wasn't taking her to meet you after all. She became hostile toward him, screaming and demanding to be returned to the marina. He responded by raping her and strangling her to death on your uncle's boat. Emily must have put up a fight because, unnoticed by Russell, her necklace came off during the struggle."

I began to cry again but this time Dr. Ruben continued without stopping. "Russell then dumped Emily's body on the northwest side of the uninhabited island in the Amelia River, before taking the boat back to the marina and putting the spare key back under your uncle's plant pot. What Russell didn't know, however, was that when he folded those blankets and put them away, back into storage, he had also hidden away a piece of evidence that you would eventually find and that linked him to Emily's murder.

"You see, when you were arrested, your uncle was arrested shortly after, since you told the police you had found the necklace on his boat. In custody, your uncle told the police that those blankets had been on his boat for many, many years. He admitted that they probably needed a wash, but that he himself would only ever take out the top one on rare occasions. It was only because you took out the top two blankets that you found the necklace."

Finally, Dr. Ruben stopped speaking and I looked at her through my tears and managed to stop crying. After a few moments of silence, she pressed the stop button on the tape recorder and ejected the tape. She then said, "You must be wondering why I am telling you all of this, how I am even allowed to tell you." Her tone of voice became a little softer as she continued. "Well, technically I am not, but the murder of Emily Hobson left a large scar on the community of Amelia Island. It caused heartache and embarrassment for the local law enforcement community as well, especially since she was the daughter of a local policeman, and they hadn't been able to find her murderer in all these years.

"Now, however, the police are more than confident, as am I, that they have arrested the right person, Russell Keeler, for her murder. The only concern they have is the way in which the necklace was found. Your story, that you met Emily by the marina and took her for a boat ride, and that you believed she left the necklace on the boat for you. That story could open up a whole can of worms for the prosecution team when the case goes to trial. Yes, there is also extremely strong DNA evidence, but Russell could change his story, say the sex was consensual, say that he left her alive by the marina after taking her out on your uncle's boat.

"No one in the community wants any surprises when this case goes to trial, Jonathan." Dr. Ruben's voice sounded caring as she spoke, and was mirrored by her demeanor, but I was now getting the impression that it was, and always had been, to lead me somewhere: for Dr. Ruben to achieve some goal she had set out for. "Now," she said, "I told you that I was on your side and I am. My professional assessment is that you were in a temporary delusional state when you say you took Emily for a boat ride. Temporary being the important word in that statement." She stopped speaking and looked at me. I wasn't sure if there was a hidden threat in what she was saying. "Also," she added, "there is the matter of the marijuana that was found in your backpack. Now, as you have pointed out, when the police arrested you there were some procedural irregularities: you not having your rights read to you immediately and you being handled a little roughly while being arrested. So, it's fair to say the police have also made some mistakes.

"As a way to try and put things right, for you and for this community, the police are willing to forget about finding the marijuana in your backpack. For my part, I have no reason to believe you are not in a sound mental state, providing you promise to quit smoking marijuana. In return, however, the police and this community would expect you to change your statement about how you found the necklace.

"You will say that you went to your uncle's boat, took the boat out onto the river alone and when you returned to the marina and moored it, you removed the blankets from storage, one to put over your shoulders to keep warm, and one to sit on. You wanted to take in the fresh air and look up at the sky and that's when the necklace fell out of the second blanket you unfolded and onto the deck.

"You will say you recognized it from an online news article about the case you happened to read about six months ago. That's six months before now. You took an interest in what the article said because the disappearance and murder of this girl, in the article you read, happened close to where your uncle lives. You remembered the necklace clearly from photos of it that were in this online news article. You only learned that you were the young man the police had been looking for back in 2009 after Russell Keeler was arrested. The fact that police had been looking for a young man in connection to Emily's murder back then was not mentioned in this online news article, and you were not aware of it at the time, which is true, otherwise you would have come forward. You will be provided with a web address for an actual news article to read that fits what I am telling you.

"You will say that you didn't touch the necklace when you discovered it, and because your cellphone battery was dead, you walked back to your uncle's house, took your car without informing your uncle, and drove to the local police station at Lime Street, Fernandina Beach.

"There, you explained what you had found to the desk sergeant. Then later that same evening, you went with Detective McConnaughey and Sergeant Conway to your uncle's boat to show them what you had found.

"Since then you have been with police voluntarily assisting them with their inquiries. Because the police initially suspected your uncle and raided his house, you weren't allowed to return to his home. Instead, you have been staying at this facility for your own safety. The judge's order to keep you here was in the interests of your safety only, since it is better than staying at a police station and cheaper for the taxpayer than putting you into a hotel. Finally, you have been speaking to me, voluntarily, for nothing other than counseling. The notes I have made and the tape recordings will be destroyed, just your counseling notes will remain."

Dr. Ruben stopped speaking and looked at me with a blank expression. I looked back at her without speaking and nodded. She had made it clear that the Fernandina Beach Police Department was not going to allow even the slightest chance that Russ might not be found guilty of Emily's murder due to me telling the truth about how I recalled finding Emily's necklace.

"Good," Dr. Ruben said. "Detective McConnaughey will escort you from here back to the police station." She nodded toward her office door to indicate that he was still outside. "There, you will read and sign a statement that has been prepared for you. It says what we just discussed. After that, you will be given back your things and your uncle will collect you from the station. He was released from custody yesterday and will be informed to collect you at the appropriate time. You will be given a copy of your statement so that you can become familiar with it. Once the case goes to trial you are likely to be called to testify, so make sure you are. Do you have any questions?" I shook my head but then said,

"How do you know so much about what happened to Emily, about the police investigation into her murder?"

"Very good, Jonathan," Dr. Ruben replied, "you are quite observant. I know a lot about this case because I am the criminal psychologist the police consulted after Emily's murder so that I could provide them with a psychological profile of the person that might have carried out the crime. Anything else?" I shook my head.

"Okay," Dr. Ruben said and stood up. I did the same and followed her out of the room.

I left the building and Dr. Ruben behind as I exited through a large metal and glass door, with Detective McConnaughey leading the way. He was a large, muscular man in his late 40s, and now that we were exiting the building, he was wearing a black suit jacket over his pale blue shirt that made it more obvious that he was a policeman and not a security guard. His only words to me as we left were,

"Follow me."

As we descended the shallow steps in front of the building's entrance, there at the bottom stood a middle-aged lady, short, slim and attractive. Detective McConnaughey seemed to recognize her and stopped in front of her.

"Could I have a moment to speak?" she said to him and looked at me. Detective McConnaughey turned and looked at me too, then turned back to the woman and nodded. He walked a short distance away, leaving us alone together, and sat on one of the large granite block benches that were part of the courtyard's public seating, while still keeping us squarely in his view.

"You must be Jonathan," the woman said. "I'm Emily's mother, Jayne." I was surprised and didn't know why she was here or what I should say to her, so I didn't say anything, and she started to speak again after a brief pause.

"I know about everything," she continued, "everything you told the police. I made my husband tell me all of it. I have been waiting here for you to come out. I knew they would be releasing you today.

"I wanted to tell you that I believe you. I believe you did see my Emily at the marina." Her voice became a little emotional as she spoke. "She told me about you, the night before she went missing. She told me that a handsome boy had been nice to her and had won a toy for her at the arcade, and that she was a little annoyed with herself for allowing her friends to drag her away from you before exchanging information.

"I wondered for a long time who the boy was she told me about. The boy the police couldn't locate. If he had anything to do with her murder. I know now that isn't true.

"She joked with me and her father at dinner that night, the night before she went missing, that maybe she would meet you again and you would turn out to be her knight in shining armor just like the toy you had won for her. She was right, you were, I believe that." Tears began to run down Jayne's face but she continued to talk. "There was a negative, restless energy in our home before yesterday, before Russell Keeler was arrested and charged. I felt it, but now it's gone." Emily's mother reached into her handbag and pulled out the plush knight. She placed it into my hands and made me clasp my fingers around it with her own before she resumed speaking.

"Her spirit found you that night on the marina. It led you to her necklace. She found her knight and he led the police to catch her killer. I don't believe what they tell me, that it was all in your head, that you imagined it all. She came to you, Jonathan, and you finally allowed her spirit to rest by leading the police to her killer."

8 DEADLY PASSIONS

CAST

James Quinn – Male, 35, a detective who has been working on the force for ten years.

Maria Keller – Female, 26, a detective who is new to the force, assigned with James for this first homicide case.

Ralph Stark – Male, 30, husband to the late Rachel Stark.

Harry Stein – Male, 33, forensics expert who examines dead bodies and potential crime scenes.

EXT. FRONT OF HOUSE. EVENING.
ESTABLISHING

The time is 8:06 p.m. The detectives are en route to attend the apparent homicide of Rachel Stark and they are just arriving at the house. The husband of the deceased is with other police outside of the house sitting in a police car. The head of the forensics team is already in the house.

Detectives Maria and James arrive at the scene of the crime in their car. This is Maria's first real case since she became a homicide detective.

INT. POLICE CAR. EVENING

They are sitting in the squad car talking before they go into the house.

> JAMES
> Alright Keller, so what do we know so far? Go over it with me.

> MARIA
> (Maria looks down at her notepad)
> A man, Mr. Ralph Stark, called 911 after supposedly returning from the store to find his wife dead, lying naked on the bathroom floor. No obvious signs of forced entry according to the responding officers first on the scene. Her husband is awaiting questioning and forensics are already here. Detective Johnson is heading to the store, to try and retrieve any surveillance footage that can corroborate Mr. Stark's story of being there at the time of his wife's murder.

JAMES

Good, and what are our jobs right now?

MARIA

We ask the husband some questions and examine the scene for evidence.

JAMES

Yes, we interrogate him, but what's the first rule of being a detective?

MARIA

Always keep an open mind?

JAMES

Yes, very good. We are going to ask the husband the standard questions but first, let's speak to forensics and see what they have to say. Are you ready?

MARIA

Yes, I'm ready.

JAMES

Okay, let's go.

Maria and James exit the car.

EXT. OUTSIDE FRONT OF HOUSE BY POLICE CAR THEY ARRIVED IN. EVENING

MARIA

I'm a little nervous Detective.

JAMES

Don't be nervous, you'll do fine, but I warn you that seeing a dead body can be really chilling.

MARIA
I've seen dead bodies in movies and on
TV shows, I think I'll be okay. I'm more
worried about my performance as a
detective.

JAMES
You'll be fine, just follow my lead.

MARIA
Yes sir.

James and Maria put on rubber gloves and enter the Stark
residence.

INT. BATHROOM. EVENING

HARRY
Watch your step detectives!

JAMES
I know the protocol.

HARRY
Good.

JAMES
What's the story here?

HARRY
Mrs. Stark here was stabbed in her jugular
vein. Looks like she suffered for a minute
spitting up some blood then bled out
within a few minutes. The knife appears
to be from a set of knives in the kitchen.

There was some fluid on the ground between her legs and fluid residue on her pubic area and vagina. The blacklight didn't detect any other fluid residue on her body. Samples of the fluid have been taken and swabs from the residue have also been taken. Everything is being analyzed as we speak and my team is checking for prints on the knife.

MARIA

You can do that here onsite? You don't need to take stuff back to a lab?

HARRY

You'd be surprised by the advances in mobile forensic technology.

MARIA
(Maria looks at the body.)
She looks terrible. What a horrible way to die.

HARRY

Death is rarely, if ever, pretty, but yes, she doesn't look great.

JAMES

Yes, it's horrible, but there are worse ways to go. She could have been decapitated or chopped up. Did you know that your brain is still conscious for a few minutes after you've been decapitated?

MARIA

That's doesn't bear thinking about.

HARRY

I've worked on a decapitated body before.
Were you there Quinn, on that case? A
good few years ago now.

JAMES

I think I would have remembered that.

HARRY

Ha, well you wouldn't have liked it. Very
gruesome.

JAMES

I'm sure I could handle that, but I'm not
sure about my partner here, she's new.
(James gives Maria a reassuring look.)

MARIA

You underestimate me, Quinn. I am
tougher than you think.
(Maria gives James a knowing slight
smile back.)

JAMES

I'm sure you are Keller.
(James looks at Harry.)
Anything from the husband?

HARRY

Not yet, he's outside wrapped in a mylar
blanket, sat in one of the squad cars. He
had a lot of her blood on his clothes.

JAMES

You know in cases like this, it's almost
always the husband. I'm gonna guess this
case is probably no different.

HARRY

Yes, sadly most murder victims are killed
by someone they know.

JAMES

Okay to bring him inside for questioning?

HARRY

Everything's already been photographed.
Keep him in the living room by the front
door, don't let him go any further into the
house and don't let him touch anything.

JAMES

Alright. I'll bring him in and Detective
Keller and I will ask him some questions.
Stay here Keller.

MARIA

Yes sir.

James exits.

HARRY

So, Keller, this is your first time out huh?

MARIA

Yes sir.

HARRY

Ah, well don't get cold feet over Quinn.
He's a bit of a dick sometimes but you'll
get used to him.

MARIA

I think I'll be fine with Quinn. I'm just a
little nervous.

HARRY

Yeah, I get what you mean detective.
Once we get the fingerprint results from
the knife, hopefully then we'll have a
clearer picture.

MARIA

Let's hope so, let's see what the husband
has to say.

HARRY

The husband can talk all he wants but lab
tests don't lie.
    (Maria smirks.)

Maria and Harry exit the bathroom and go to the living
room by the front door. James and Ralph Stark enter the
Stark residence.

INT. LIVING ROOM BY FRONT DOOR. EVENING

JAMES

    (Looking at Harry)
Stein, could you give us a few minutes to
talk with Mr. Stark?

HARRY

Of course detective, I should go check on
those results.

Harry exits.

JAMES

Alright, Mr. Stark, are you okay to answer
some questions?

RALPH

Yes.

JAMES

Okay, you don't have to talk to us but if you have nothing to hide and want to help us, now is the best time to talk while things are still fresh in your memory. My partner, Detective Keller, will be writing down everything that you say. We do ask that you be honest with your answers. (Looking at Maria.) Are you ready Keller?

MARIA

Yes sir, I'm ready.

JAMES

Okay Mr. Stark, explain to us what happened.

RALPH

My wife asked me to go to the store to pick up some vegetables for a stew she wanted to make. When I returned from the store and entered the house, I called out to her but she didn't answer. I put the vegetables on the kitchen counter and looked around the house. That's when I found her lying naked on the bathroom floor. There was a knife next to her body and blood all over the floor. I tried to help her, (Ralph's voice gets a little emotional.) but I knew she was dead.

JAMES

Did you notice anything out of place or unusual before you found her body? Were

any of the windows open? Was the door
unlocked?

RALPH

No, I didn't notice anything, everything
seemed normal except she didn't answer
when I called out to her. The front door
was closed and locked, I used my door
key to get in like always.

JAMES

How long were you gone for, shopping I
mean?

RALPH

Maybe half an hour, 45 minutes.

JAMES

Your clothes were covered in blood when
the police and paramedics arrived, can
you explain that?

RALPH

Yes, I got it all over me when I tried to
help her on the floor. I tried to lift her up.
I called 911, then I saw that it was her
neck that was wounded. I applied
pressure to it with my hands until the
paramedics and police arrived, but
(Ralph's voice breaks again and he tries to
compose himself.) I knew it was too late.

JAMES

Mr. Stark, did your wife ever complain to
you that someone was bothering her,
harassing her, following her? Or do you
know of anyone who might have wanted

to harm her?

RALPH
No. She was always well-liked. She got
along with everyone she knew.

JAMES
Keller, are you getting all of this?

MARIA
(Writing down on a notepad.)
Yes sir.

JAMES
Mr. Stark, what was your relationship like
with Mrs. Stark?

RALPH
We were very happy together. We wanted
to have a child, we already picked out
possible names. I loved my wife dearly.
(Ralph's voice becomes angry and
emotional.) I want her killer caught!

JAMES
Alright. We will check on the forensics
team. Mr. Stark, you may wait outside
with the officers. I will come and get you
if we have any more questions.

RALPH
Okay, thank you, detective.

Ralph exits.

JAMES
Well Keller, what do you think?

MARIA

I'm not sure yet. I think when we get the
evidence back from the forensics team,
we will be closer to knowing who killed
her.

JAMES

I think he's hiding something. His
emotional state didn't come across as
being sincere to me.

MARIA

I don't know. I wouldn't jump to
conclusions just yet.

JAMES

I'm normally pretty good with my
hunches.

MARIA

Well, we'll see.

Harry enters the Stark residence holding up a clear
forensics bag containing a knife.

JAMES

What did you find Dr. Stein?

HARRY

It seems we have a bit of a mystery. There
were no prints found on the knife,
however, the liquid that we found turns
out to be semen. So that could explain
why she was naked when we found her.

JAMES

She had intercourse before she died?

HARRY

The swabs from her pubic region and vulva were also positive for semen. The vaginal swabs didn't find any semen deep inside and no obvious signs of force. Her genitals were recently shaven, I'm guessing that's just how she kept herself, the husband should be able to confirm that. If I had to guess I would say the murderer ejaculated onto her dead body, onto her pubic bone. It's possible we could be looking at rape and then murder, maybe he pulled out, but if that were the case, we'd expect to see a wider area in which the blacklight would have detected semen. And another thing, her clothes were in the bathtub. They were folded and placed into it neatly.

MARIA

That's unusual, what could that mean?

JAMES

So, no semen on the inside of her vagina?

HARRY

The swabs came back positive only at the very opening. I think the murderer ejaculated onto her pubic bone and it ran down and pooled between her legs.

MARIA

Has Mr. Stark consented to having his DNA taken?

HARRY

Yes, he consented to be swabbed.

MARIA

How long will it take for the results to come back?

HARRY

These new mobile testing labs are amazing. The results should be back at any moment.

MARIA

And there were no prints on the knife?

HARRY

No, detective. The murderer left his semen and therefore DNA behind, but was careful enough to make sure there were no prints on the knife, which seems somewhat odd. Let me go and check on those DNA results.

Harry exits the house.

MARIA

That is kind of strange don't you think?

JAMES

Maybe, maybe not. Perhaps he wore gloves and had no intention of ejaculating but couldn't control himself. Maybe Mr. Stark and his wife were playing a sex game that went wrong.

MARIA

What do you mean, sex game?

JAMES

You know, it happens all of the time.

Bored couple, trying to spice things up,
he plays the burglar breaking in, she plays
the defenseless housewife, maybe he took
it too far.

Harry reenters the room holding up a sheet of paper.

HARRY
You're not going to believe this. The
DNA from the semen is a match for Mr.
Stark's DNA.

JAMES
I knew it!

MARIA
We should ask him more questions. Right
Detective Quinn?
(Maria looks at James for approval.)

JAMES
Yes, I'll go and get him.

James exits the Stark Residence.

MARIA
Something is wrong. Why would he
consent to giving his DNA? He must
have known we'd match the semen to
him?

HARRY
Refusing would make him look guilty, he
knows that. He had no choice.

James and Ralph Stark enter the Stark Residence.

JAMES

Dr. Stein, could you give us a moment
alone so we may talk with Mr. Stark?

HARRY

Yes of course. I have some more work to
do anyway.

Harry exits the Stark residence.

JAMES

Okay, Mr. Stark, we would like to ask you
some more questions. Is that alright with
you?

RALPH

Yes, but I don't know what else I can tell
you. I have told you everything.

MARIA

Mr. Stark, some of the forensic results
have come back. Semen consistent with
your DNA profile was on your wife's
body. Did you have sexual relations with
your wife before she died, before you
went to the store to pick up the
vegetables?

RALPH

(Angrily) What! No! We didn't have sex
before she died. What the hell are you
talking about!

JAMES

When was the last time you had sex with
your wife, Mr. Stark?

RALPH

I don't know, about a week ago, I think.

MARIA

That doesn't seem possible though, does it, Mr. Stark? How is it possible that you had sex a week ago and yet the forensics team has found your semen on your wife's body today?

RALPH

I don't know, there must be some sort of mistake!

JAMES

I am arresting you on suspicion of murdering your wife. You have the right to remain silent. Anything you say can and will be used against you in a court of law. You have the right to an attorney and if you cannot afford an attorney, one will be appointed for you. Do you understand?

RALPH

(In an angry and surprised voice) This is crazy! I didn't do anything, I'm going to sue!

JAMES

Turn around and put your hands behind your back.

Ralph does as he is told and James handcuffs him.

MARIA

(Whispers into James's ear) Sir, something

doesn't feel right. Give me ten more
minutes to look around.

JAMES
Fine, you have ten minutes, but it's time
to wrap this up. I'll be outside in the car.

MARIA
Send Harry back in for me.

JAMES
Alright but make this quick.

MARIA
(To herself, under her breath) There's got
to be more here.

James leads Ralph out of the house. Maria looks around
the house, entering the bedroom.

INT. BEDROOM. EVENING

Harry enters the bedroom.

HARRY
What is it? Quinn said you wanted to see
me?

MARIA
I don't know, something doesn't feel right
about this case. Just wanted your thoughts
on the matter.

Before Harry can reply Maria opens an underwear drawer,
seemingly belonging to Mrs. Stark, and finds a receipt for a
restaurant dated from the previous week.

HARRY

What have you got there?

MARIA

A receipt from a restaurant dated last week. It was in the wife's underwear drawer.

Maria places the receipt inside an evidence bag with her gloved hand.

HARRY

Doesn't seem like anything important.

MARIA

But why would she keep this in her underwear drawer?

HARRY

Beats me, but I think you are right about things not adding up. I found something odd.

MARIA

Yes?

HARRY

More analysis has come back on the semen. Not a single sperm was moving.

MARIA

What does that mean?

HARRY

Well, the pool of semen on the floor hadn't dried out. Taking into account the temperature of the room and the

estimated time of death, you would
expect to find some of the sperm
showing signs of movement, but there's
not a single hint of it from the
microscopic analysis.

MARIA

So, what's it mean?

HARRY

So, it's possible the semen was old, like it
had been stored somewhere and then
placed on her. Had the semen completely
dried out, we would never have
discovered that.

MARIA

You think someone was trying to frame
Mr. Stark? Who? How would they have
got hold of his semen?

HARRY

I don't know but it's a possibility.

MARIA

Help me look around some more. Quinn
wants to wrap this up, but I think... We
both think, there's more going on here.

Maria and Harry search the house. They
then reenter the bathroom.

INT. BATHROOM. EVENING

MARIA

What's that in the toilet?

HARRY
(Looking down into the toilet)
I think it's a pill bottle. How the hell did
my guys miss that! Someone's going to
get a stern talking to!

MARIA
What would a pill bottle be doing in the
toilet? Unless someone was trying to flush
it.

Harry takes photos of the pill bottle and then picks it up
with a gloved hand and takes off the lid.

HARRY
I don't know. There's no label and it
looks like there's more semen inside of
the bottle. I'll get this checked out.

MARIA
Alright, go do whatever it is you do. Let
Quinn know about the possibility of old
semen being deliberately placed onto her
and what we found in the toilet, and ask
him to come back in. I'll be in the living
room by the front door.

Maria exits the bathroom with Harry. Harry exits the
house. A few moments later James enters the living room.

INT. LIVING ROOM BY FRONT DOOR - EVENING

JAMES
What did you find?

MARIA

I found a receipt for Anthony's Organic Restaurant. It's an expensive Italian restaurant in town, I happen to know of it. The receipt was in Mrs. Stark's underwear drawer, dated last week, and Stein told you about the unmarked pill bottle we found in the toilet with more semen inside of it.

JAMES

Okay, so where are you going with this?

MARIA

I don't know but we need to ask him more questions.

JAMES

He isn't going to talk to us now.

MARIA

Let me try.

JAMES

Alright, but this better be going somewhere.

James exits and returns with Mr. Stark.

MARIA

Listen, Mr. Stark, I want to help you. I don't think you killed your wife. You don't have to answer what I am going to ask you, but if you do, we might be able to clear this up right away. We also have someone on their way to the store you shopped at, to retrieve the camera footage

and confirm you were there at the time
your wife was killed. Please help me help
you.

RALPH

I have told you everything.

MARIA

Please Mr. Stark.

RALPH

(Sternly) Okay, ask me!

MARIA

Thank you. Mr. Stark, we found this
receipt for Anthony's Organic Restaurant,
dated from last week, in your wife's
bedside underwear drawer. Do you know
why your wife kept this receipt and put it
in her underwear drawer?

RALPH

Okay, okay. My wife and I were not
happy. We've been fighting on and off for
months and I just wasn't happy with her
anymore. That dinner wasn't with my
wife, it was with my lover. I've been
having an affair for a few months now, I
was planning on leaving her. My wife
must have found the receipt. I was
beginning to suspect she knew about the
affair, but you have to believe me, I didn't
kill her!

MARIA

We also found a pill bottle, a small orange
one. Are you taking any medication? Or

was your wife?

RALPH
That sounds like a bottle of my wife's antidepressants. She's had depression and anxiety since the breakdown of our relationship.

Harry pokes his head through the front door.

HARRY
Detective Keller, could you come out here with me for a minute?

MARIA
Yes.

Maria walks out to the van with Harry.

EXT. OUTSIDE FRONT OF HOUSE BY POLICE FORENSICS MOBILE LAB VAN. EVENING

HARRY
It was Mr. Stark's semen in the pill bottle, and again the sperm were completely dead. Although, if that semen was placed into that bottle around the estimated time of death, then we are now right on the borderline of where we would expect to observe any sperm cells still moving.

MARIA
That is interesting. I think I have an idea of what happened, but let me talk to Quinn first.

Maria returns to the living room.

INT. LIVING ROOM BY FRONT DOOR. EVENING

JAMES
Detective Keller, did you want to ask any
more questions of Mr. Stark?

MARIA
No, I think I have everything I need. Mr.
Stark, please wait with the officers outside
while I talk with my partner?

Ralph exits the house. An officer standing outside of the
front door takes Mr. Stark to wait by a police car.

JAMES
Alright, what have you got Keller?

MARIA
Here's what I think. I think that Rachel
Stark found the receipt, and had known
for a while that her husband was having
an affair and was planning on leaving her.
I think that she had sex with her husband
last week, just like Mr. Stark told us, and
she saved the semen until this week using
one of her empty pill bottles. Then this
evening she told her husband to go out to
the store to get vegetables for a stew she
wanted to cook. While he was gone she
stripped naked, folded her clothes neatly
and put them into the bathtub, got a knife
from the kitchen, took the pill bottle full
of her husband's semen, laid on the floor,
and poured the semen onto her genital
area. Then she closed the pill bottle,

threw it into the toilet behind her head, and stabbed herself in the neck while covering the knife handle with a tissue. She then dropped the knife, threw the tissue into the toilet and flushed it. The tissue flushed but the pill bottle floated and she bled to death on the bathroom floor. She committed suicide, but pinned it on her husband so that he wouldn't get to be with his lover. What do you think?

                    JAMES
What do I think? That's the most fantastical story I have ever heard. I think that it's a crazy idea, but I have to admit it fits the evidence.

Harry enters the house.

                    HARRY
I have some news. Detective Johnson just got back from the store. Their store's surveillance cameras haven't been working, but when Detective Johnson showed Mr. Stark's photo to the counter clerk, she remembered serving him. She said she remembered him because he complimented her on her hair.

Maria and James leave the house and go to Ralph, by the police car.

EXT. OUTSIDE FRONT OF HOUSE BY POLICE
VEHICLES. EVENING

                    JAMES
Okay, listen Mr. Stark. This is going to

sound very odd, but we now have reason
to believe your wife had discovered your
affair and that you were planning on
leaving her. We think she killed herself
and tried to make it look like you did it.

RALPH
(Shocked voice.) Oh my god, Rachel?
Why? This is my fault. I knew she was
depressed but I never thought… (Voice
trails off while Ralph shakes his head.)

James uncuffs Ralph.

JAMES
We are still going to have to process you
down at the station.

RALPH
I understand. May I please make a phone
call? My mother was supposed to be
visiting us tomorrow. She doesn't know
what's happened. Please, I don't want her
to leave home, she's elderly and she'll be
catching a flight in the next few hours. I
don't want her to arrive to all of this.

JAMES
We're not supposed to do this, but okay,
you have been through a terrible event.

James retrieves Ralph's phone from an evidence bag in
the police van and hands it to him.

JAMES
Be quick.

Ralph takes the phone and walks a few steps away from the detectives, then dials a number.

RALPH
(Quietly into the phone.) Honey, the plan worked. They think she killed herself. I told you they would come by the store. You told them exactly what they needed to hear. I couldn't wait to tell you. I have to delete this number from the phone's history now and then call my mother. I'll explain later. I love you.

Made in the USA
Middletown, DE
11 December 2020

27275217R00113